Miracles never happen to
INVISIBLE GIRL.

"I'm not going to Danica's party."

"Not going?" Bernadette was aghast.

"You're the one that said Danica only invited me because she wanted someone to do her homework."

"I was mad," she muttered. "I'm sorry. You should go, Julep. I'm dying to know what her house looks like inside. You just gotta go and tell me everything. And I mean everything."

"It would take a miracle for me to go to that party. A miracle."

And as anyone could tell you, miracles did not happen to Invisible Girl.

Julep wanted to change the subject. Now. "So are you going T.O.T.-ing with your cousins?" she asked Bernadette.

"Maybe. I heard Mrs. Wiley is giving out giant Hershey bars, so I might go up to Bridle Trails and do the circle."

"Bern," Julep cut her off. "I have to go."

"What's wrong?"

"It's Cooper."

Her friend let out a hearty laugh. "What's he done this time?"

Julep stared at the pale, grape-juice-stained face of the boy standing in the kitchen doorway. Cooper was holding Fred against his heaving chest.

"He's having an asthma attack," Julep croaked. "A bad one."

Books by Trudi Trueit

Julep O'Toole: Confessions of a Middle Child

Julep O'Toole: Miss Independent

Julep O'Toole

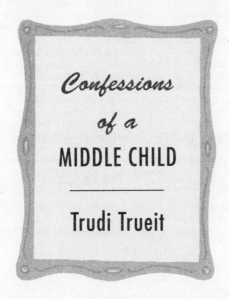

Confessions

of a

MIDDLE CHILD

Trudi Trueit

PUFFIN BOOKS

PUFFIN BOOKS
Published by the Penguin Group
Penguin Young Readers Group, 345 Hudson Street, New York, New York 10014, U.S.A.
Penguin Group (Canada), 90 Eglinton Avenue East, Suite 700,
Toronto, Ontario, Canada M4P 2Y3 (a division of Pearson Penguin Canada Inc.)
Penguin Books Ltd, 80 Strand, London WC2R 0RL, England
Penguin Ireland, 25 St Stephen's Green, Dublin 2, Ireland
(a division of Penguin Books Ltd)
Penguin Group (Australia), 250 Camberwell Road, Camberwell, Victoria 3124, Australia
(a division of Pearson Australia Group Pty Ltd)
Penguin Books India Pvt Ltd, 11 Community Centre,
Panchsheel Park, New Delhi - 110 017, India
Penguin Group (NZ), Cnr Airborne and Rosedale Roads,
Albany, Auckland 1310, New Zealand (a division of Pearson New Zealand Ltd)
Penguin Books (South Africa) (Pty) Ltd, 24 Sturdee Avenue,
Rosebank, Johannesburg 2196, South Africa

Registered Offices: Penguin Books Ltd, 80 Strand, London WC2R 0RL, England

First published in the United States of America by Dutton Children's Books,
a division of Penguin Young Readers Group, 2005
Published by Puffin Books, a division of Penguin Young Readers Group, 2007

10 9 8 7 6 5 4 3 2 1

CIP Data is available.
ISBN: 978-0-525-47619-9 (hardcover)

Puffin Books ISBN 978-0-14-240798-1

Designed by Irene Vandervoort
Printed in the United States of America

*To my parents, for helping their middle child
discover she wasn't invisible, after all*

Contents

Julep O'Toole

Confessions

of a

MIDDLE CHILD

1 INVISIBLE GIRL

Julep stared at the worn carpet less than an inch from her silver toenails. It was a color that could only be described in two words: *dog doo*. Spots of grape juice, pizza sauce, and some yellowish blobs she couldn't identify winked at her. They dared her to hop through the maze of stains without touching them.

"No way," she said, backing up in case the carpet made a sudden grab for her ankle.

Eleven-year-old Julep had always done her best to stay far, far away from her brother's room, a.k.a. the Chicken Coop. The place smelled like her mother's rhubarb-beet-asparagus meatless burgers (with pimentos—gag) and looked a whole lot worse. Old, torn pieces of masking tape, rusted tacks, and bent nails clung to the snot-green walls. The once powder-white vinyl blinds had faded to a dingy yellow. The strings were tangled into a jumble of knots the size of a baseball. The blinds hung lopsidedly over a window smeared with hundreds of dirty fingerprints—every single one of them belonging to Cooper

Maynard O'Toole, the biggest pain-in-the-rumpus little brother ever to exist in the solar system.

The place was ugly. It was stinky. And now, unfortunately, it was all hers.

What's that black goo in the corner?

Julep pulled a lock of wavy, light reddish-brown hair over her eyes. Some things were best left unexplored.

How did this happen? Julep couldn't believe that she'd agreed to swap rooms with her seven-year-old brother. The whole thing had landed with a splat in her lap like a huge ostrich egg—one gigantic, rotten egg that she had never seen flying through the air toward her, though she really ought to have been paying closer attention. Stuff like this was always happening to her.

"Carpets trap dirt, dust mites, pollen, and all kinds of things," Allison Gallardo-O'Toole had told her daughter as they'd driven home from the grocery store one drizzly Saturday morning in late September.

"They do?" Julep didn't know what a dust mite was. She didn't have a carpet in her bedroom, so why worry about something you've never heard of trapped in something you didn't have?

Julep turned to watch a row of maple trees whiz past, their leaves tipped in autumn red. Fall was her favorite time of the year. Halloween was more than a month away, but Julep could hardly wait. Carving pumpkins. Making caramel apples. Getting tons of chocolate. Who didn't love it? Julep's favorite part was choosing a costume that would transform her into someone famous, beautiful, or heroic—anyone other than who she truly was.

On every other day of the year Julep was—oh, how she cringed at the word—average. She wasn't a walking brain, yet she could hold her own for a few rounds in a spelling bee. She couldn't hit a home run most times she came up to bat, but she wasn't afraid to stick her mitt out to catch a fly ball. Julep's voice wasn't going to win praise from Simon on *American Idol.* Still, her friends didn't plug their ears when she sang. Yep, that was the tragedy that was her life. Julep wasn't good enough to be noticed, and she wasn't bad enough to be noticed. She was, as her former ice-skating instructor had put it, "unexceptional."

Ouch.

More than anything, Julep felt . . . transparent. This was especially true when it came to her family. Her parents, older sister, and younger brother often stared right through her. They talked at her, around her, and about her but rarely *to* her. Julep was, now that she thought about it, a lot like air: there but not there.

She was Julep Antoinette O'Toole, Invisible Girl.

Julep wondered if there were any Halloween costumes that made a middle child visible. Somehow she doubted it.

"The doctor says it would be better for Cooper's allergies if he had a hardwood floor," her mother had said as she turned onto Bayview Drive. She stole a quick glance in Julep's direction. "He says it can make a big difference in cutting down asthma attacks."

"Uh-huh." Julep was pretending to use her mind to blow the beads of water diagonally across the car window. She wondered if her mother had remembered to buy her favorite Lorna Doone cookies. Probably not. Julep glanced in the backseat to see the top of a Pringles can sticking out of a bag. Pringles were Harmony's favorite. It figured. Invisible Girl had been overlooked again, while her older sister, Miss Perfect, got everything *she* wanted.

"We managed to buy the air filter for the house, a new mattress and cover for Cooper's bed, and the new vacuum with the HEPA filter, so . . ." Her mother trailed off, tapping the steering wheel with her thumbs. "We thought . . . your dad and I thought that rather than laying a completely new hardwood floor and spending more money, especially with your dad out of work right now . . . uh, it would be easier to . . . I mean, since you already have a birch floor and everything, it might be simplest for you to trade rooms with Cooper."

Julep swiveled around so fast a cramp sliced through her left shoulder blade. "Trade rooms?" She winced, not from the pain, but from the thought of actually living in the totally disgusting, rancid-smelling, bacteria-growing Chicken Coop.

"We're all making small sacrifices. . . ."

Small? SMALL? Was her mother kidding? A small sacrifice was taking a shorter shower or turning off lights around the house to save money on the utility bill. Giving up her room definitely fit under the heading of *colossal* sacrifice.

Wait a second. Something was wrong here.

Julep narrowed her eyes. "What is Harmony giving up?"

"Your sister? Uh . . . well . . ." Her mother twisted her lips.

Julep knew it! Gritting her teeth, she asked, "Why can't *she* give up her room?"

"Well, Harmony has carpeting, hon."

There was always a reason why Harmony got her way. She was fourteen and the oldest of the three O'Toole kids. She got to wear makeup. And perfume. Her hair didn't come in a thick lump the color of a terra-cotta pot that flipped under when you wanted it to go over and over when you wanted it to go under. Harmony's honey-blond hair, streaked with golden rays of sunshine, always hung perfectly straight down her back. Always. You couldn't play connect the dots with the freckles on Harmony's face, because she didn't have any. Not a single one. Julep had eighty-seven freckles splashed across her nose and cheeks. Eighty-seven little brown dots you couldn't wash or wish away, no matter how hard you tried. Everyone loved Harmony Elizabeth O'Toole. She was perfect. That's what teachers, parents, coaches, kids, and even strangers on the street were forever saying to Julep. "You must feel so lucky to have a sister who's so perfect," they'd say.

Uh-huh. Real lucky. Gag-o-matic. You try using the bathroom after Miss Perfect has gelled, moussed, hair-sprayed, and powdered herself for the day.

Why should her sister get to be beautiful, talented, smart, *and* be able to keep her room? It wasn't fair. Julep let her mother continue telling her about how a hardwood floor would help Cooper's asthma, but inside her mind, the word kept flashing neon blue: No. NO. *NO!*

She didn't say it, though, because it wouldn't have mattered. That's what it was like when you were little more than a puff of air. People couldn't see you. Couldn't touch you. Couldn't hear you. What you thought didn't count for squat.

"So what do you think?" her mom asked, not taking her eyes off the road.

Julep could fight it, but, in the end, she knew she would lose. There was no point in sharing her opinion because nobody was going to listen to her anyway. Defeated, she turned to draw a sad face in the steam on her window. "Okay," Julep murmured.

She barely felt her mother pat her knee. "Maybe you'd like to do something special with Trig or Bernadette this weekend? I could rent a movie for you."

Julep shook her head.

"Mukilteo Beach?"

While it was certainly fun to have seagulls dive-bomb you for your Doritos, it couldn't begin to make up for losing the one place in the world that was truly and completely yours.

"How about some pizza? I've got a coupon for a large at Luigi's. We could get the veggie special with tomatoes, mushrooms, and roasted zucchini. . . ."

Soggy zucchini? Was she serious? Julep's sandals tasted better than that stuff. But when your mom is a vegetarian, like it or not, so are you. How could anyone eat vegetable pizza? If you couldn't have pepperoni, then it seemed like a waste of perfectly good cheese, sauce, and dough to Julep.

"No, thanks," Julep whispered, suddenly feeling tired.

"Think about it," her mom said softly. "If there's something you'd like, something not too expensive, let me know, okay?"

Julep let her forehead fall against the car window. There *was* something, but . . .

Last week, she'd seen an adorable watch at Mulberry Lane, her favorite gift shop in the mall. It had a hinged mother-of-pearl oval cover that you flipped up when you wanted to see what time it was. Inside, teeny pink rhinestones took the place of the numbers on the pearly white face. The stretchy-silver band held clumps of pink, purple, and clear beads, along with several silver roses. The moment Julep slipped it on, the faceted beads caught the sunlight and painted mini-rainbows on her wrist. Julep had been admiring it when Harmony grabbed her hand. "Dream on," she'd said, shaking her perfect hair. "It's forty dollars."

If business hadn't been so slow and Julep's dad hadn't had to close his software-design company three months ago, she might have asked for the watch. But not now. Thank goodness her mother still had her public-relations job at the Seattle Art Museum. Even so, with the family down to one income, everybody had to watch their spending. "Too expensive" was

Mom-speak for anything over ten dollars. What decent thing could you possibly buy for less than ten dollars? Nothing good. Okay, food. You could buy food. But Julep had just lost her beloved bedroom. And with it her appetite. She would never eat again. Never. Well, at least, nothing with soggy bits of zucchini in it.

A girl's got to have her limits. Even if she *is* invisible.

6:59 P.M.   Mood: furious

EMERGENCY JOURNAL ENTRY

Dear Journal:

Bad news. I have to trade rooms with Cooper. Are you okay? I'm definitely not. I need those electric paddles that start your heart 'cause I am in total and complete shock. CLEAR!

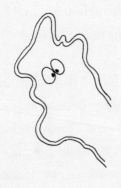

There's mold growing in the Coop that science hasn't identified. Not that my mom and dad care that I'm going to have to live in it. All they care about is Cooper's health. That's what happens when you are an M.M.M.C. (see decoder page). It's J.I.C.A.R.T. (again, check the decoder page).

Bernadette says if you believe something with all your heart and focus all your energy on it and put every bit of brain power you have into it, then it has to come true. Okay, here goes . . .

I won't have to live in the Chicken Coop.

  I won't have to live in the Chicken Coop.

    <u>I won't have to live in the Chicken Coop.</u>

I have to go to the store. You're going to need more pages.

W.A.N.!

C.Y.L.

Love,

Julep, M.M.M.C.

Julep's Secret Decoder Page

PRIVATE!   STOP READING NOW!

M.M.M.C.: Miserable Misunderstood Middle Child

J.I.C.A.R.T.: Just In Case Anybody Reads This

W.A.N.: What A Nightmare

C.Y.L.: Check You Later

MAY ANYONE WHO READS THIS GET
V.Z. (VOLCANIC ZITS)!

2 The Chicken Coop

Julep awoke one Saturday morning in early October to odd scraping noises outside her bedroom. Rubbing her eyes and yawning, she slid out of bed and stumbled to the door to tell Cooper to go away. When she opened it, nobody was there; however, the vacuum cleaner and mop were resting side by side against the hallway wall next to her door. Stacks of toys and games blocked the narrow path to her brother's room.

Julep flung her door shut and threw her back against it.

This was it!

Swapping day. Her heart began to pound faster.

Frantic, Julep shoved her desk chair under the doorknob to keep anyone from entering. She needed time to think of a plan to hang on to her precious bedroom. Lots of time. She had barely pulled on a pair of jeans and her gray University of Washington T-shirt when someone knocked on her door.

"Julep?" It was her dad.

The doorknob jiggled.

"Wake up, hon. It's time to move," her mother said.

Julep's bare feet froze to her hardwood floor. If she didn't say a thing or move a muscle, they might go away.

She could hear her parents talking. "There's something blocking the door. . . ."

"Is she even in there?"

"She's in there."

"Julep, open this door right now," her father said firmly.

It was hopeless. She could hold out for three, maybe four hours, but eventually her bladder would betray her. She would have to whiz, and then they would have her. There was nothing Julep could do to stop the injustice. And so she did what anyone in her position would do. Julep surrendered before she got grounded for the remainder of middle school.

Good-bye, buttercup yellow walls.

Good-bye, bay window.

Good-bye, shiny birchwood floor.

Hello, disgusting Chicken Coop.

Life was so not fair. She hoped Harmony hadn't eaten all of the chocolate donuts. Julep was going to need at least two to make it through this morning.

As her parents helped her move into her brother's room, Julep comforted herself with the knowledge that her co-best friends, Bernadette and Trig, had promised to come to her rescue. They were going to help her redecorate the Coop. Although she wondered if it was truly possible to fix the place. Just unraveling the cord to the venetian blinds could take decades. And what was she supposed to do about the dog-doo carpet and snot-green walls? Two words came to mind: *complete demolition*.

By noon, the move was almost complete, and Julep was exhausted. Who knew you could pack so much junk into one closet? Between the hordes of stuffed animals, old games, puzzles, and clothes, she had no idea she owned so much stuff. Her mother suggested she make a "giveaway" pile. No way. She'd given up enough already. Julep vowed to keep everything, including one red-and-green plaid sock that had lost its mate, a Yahtzee game with only three dice, and a bald Barbie doll (poor thing—Cooper had given her a buzz cut). Julep might never give up anything ever again.

Deal with that.

"Your dad and I are going to run a few errands and pick up lunch," said her mom, passing Julep in the hall for the hundredth time. "We'll move your bed and dresser when we get back. Harmony's in charge while we're gone."

Julep crossed one eyeball in. Her older sister always enjoyed ordering Julep around when their parents weren't home. "Make me a cinnamon toast," she'd order, "and don't forget the chocolate milk." When you were the oldest, you got to do that kind of thing to torture your middle-child sister. Julep was pretty certain it said so in the *Nasty Big Sister Rule Book.*

When Julep sauntered into her room—or what used to be her room—she caught Cooper bouncing on her buttercup-yellow velvet bedspread, trying to yank her ballerina poster off the wall.

"Stop," she shouted. "You'll tear it."

"Will not," snapped Cooper as they both heard a corner rip.

"Let it go, and get your crusty tennis shoes off my bed."

"You're not the boss of me," he spit, though he did release the poster.

Julep caught it to keep it from ripping further. Carefully, she removed the tacks from the wall and lowered the poster to the floor. A tiny piece of the corner was torn, but a little tape would repair it. As Julep was gently rolling up the poster, she saw her brother's small, wiry body stretching across the bay window. Julep had cracked open the last section of the window to let in some air, and it had started to rain. Now the inside of the ledge was dotted with raindrops. A small cardboard box Julep had packed with some of her most important belongings was also on the ledge. It was getting wet, too.

Dirty fingers were reaching for the white curtain rod.

"It's slippery," she warned, trying to copy her mother's stern tone. "Move my box out of the rain, please. . . . Cooper, are you listening to me? I said leave those alone."

"No way am I keeping up some dumb daisy curtains."

"I'll get them down in a minute," she said with a glare, "and I'm not going to tell you again to get off my bed." She was losing her patience. Julep was giving up her room for him, and he was being a total goober. He didn't care about her sacrifice. He had never even bothered to say "Thanks" for all that she was doing for him.

"Get off or else," threatened Julep, feeling a tingle at the top of her scalp. Her hair always itched whenever she got mad. Follicles of Fury, Trig called them.

Her brother quit jumping, but he didn't get off the mattress. "Or else what?" He tipped his head, and a lock of uncombed, pale-blond hair fell into his eyes. To tease her, Cooper stuck his foot out and tapped Julep's box that was sitting on the ledge. Julep could see the corner of her purple journal sticking up out of the box, along with the end of the rectangular blue plastic box where she kept her hair clips and bands. A petite straw hat with an orange ribbon told Julep that her favorite stuffed animal, a calico cat named Katie, was also tucked inside the box.

With an evil smirk, her brother pushed the box a little harder. On the slick ledge, it easily glided several inches. Now one corner was sticking out beyond the edge of the window.

"Cooper," she growled.

"What?" He feigned innocence.

"Don't you dare," she said, immediately regretting the words. Daring Cooper to do or not do something was inviting trouble. He didn't like to lose, and he rarely backed down. The only way to win now was to force a stalemate. Quickly, she glanced around. Julep grabbed one of her brother's model airplanes. She lifted the F-14 Tomcat high above her head. "Touch it again, and I'll drop it," she said, unblinking.

"So will I." His frosty-blue eyes narrowed. With the peeling toe of one worn tennis shoe, he inched a second corner of the box until it, too, teetered over the edge. Katie's straw sun hat toppled to the floor.

Without any support beneath two of its four corners, the box began to tip.

Julep heard the pitter-pat of rain against leaves. She gulped hard.

She would have to let him have this one.

Julep set the plane on his desk and, holding her hands high, backed away. Cooper leaned forward, stumbled on the wet surface, and hit the side of the cardboard box with his left foot. For a moment, it teeter-tottered on the ledge. Julep made eye contact with Katie a second before she, and everything else in the box, fell out the window.

"Noooooo!" shrieked Julep, lunging across her bed.

Cooper peered down. "Bummer."

"Just wait until Mom and Dad get home," Julep shot over her shoulder as she raced from the room. "Cooper Maynard O'Toole, you are in sooooo much trouble . . . so much trouble. . . ."

Once outside, Julep began scooping up her belongings before the rain could soak them through. Her plastic case had landed on the picnic table. A long crack had etched its way across the side, and the latch was broken. Julep scrambled around the backyard, plucking sequined hair clips, ponytail bands, and glittery barrettes out of the grass and lavender hedge. She also saved a few pages of loose artwork that had been tucked into the back of her journal, though she knew the rain had probably ruined them. Some of her colored pens had landed in the roses. A pretty teacup night-light that her aunt had given her for her birthday had shattered into a gazillion pieces on the wood deck. Picking up the broken china, Julep threw them in the big gray trash bin. She wiped tears from her eyes, determined not to let her brother see her cry. Could this day get any worse?

After several minutes of scavenging for her things, Julep still had not found Katie or her journal. Sniffling, she glanced up. A big raindrop sploshed into her right eyeball. When she'd wiped her eyes, Julep looked up again, following the line from her old bay window straight down to—

Rats!

There was only one place her favorite stuffed kitty and journal could be: in the giant holly bush. Undaunted, Julep pried a couple of thick branches apart and stepped into the bush. The second she let the branches go, they snapped back into place. Thousands of thorny leaves dug into her arms.

"Ow . . . ow," she cried, trying to untangle herself from the razor-sharp bush.

This was not going to work. She could wait until her parents got home, but by then Katie would be drenched, and her journal would be nothing but a gloppy mess of paper and ink. Julep pushed a wet strand of hair out of her eyes. It was starting to rain harder. She had better do something. And fast.

Julep circled the giant fortress of a bush once, then turned and circled in the other direction. She munched off the first two fingernails on her right hand. She was working on the third fingernail when she got an idea. Julep hurried into the house, collected everything she needed, and prepared for her mission. It would have been a brilliant plan, too, had it not been for one unexpected and ill-timed arrival.

Julep was coming out of the holly bush, feeling quite proud of herself for retrieving Katie and her journal intact, when Calvin Kapinski rolled past on his skateboard. He didn't say a word, but by his furrowed eyebrows and O-shaped mouth, Julep knew the news would be all over Heatherwood Middle School in less than twenty-four hours.

After all, what can you say when the most obnoxious kid in school catches you wearing your dad's yellow hip-wader fishing boots, your mom's puffy red ski parka, a couple of rainbow-trout oven mitts, and a purple towel over your head held on by a pair of swimming goggles? No, there's really nothing you can say. All you can do is shriek until your hair falls out, run behind the lavender hedge, and pray to die right then and there.

Which is exactly what Julep did.

Only after she had made certain Calvin was gone and no one else was around did Julep slip out from behind the lavender. She looked up. Her goggles were starting to fog over, and the rain blurred her vision. She couldn't see her little brother, but Julep could certainly hear him. Cooper was howling like crazy. He had seen everything.

"You'll regret this, Cooper Maynard O'Toole," snarled Julep, reaching up to rip the goggles off her head. Her oven mitt slipped, and the goggles snapped back against her face. A tidal waved of pain surged through her forehead.

Suddenly, a white haze was choking her. Julep flung her arms up to escape the wispy web before it occurred to her she was fighting off her white daisy curtains—two more victims of one pain-in-the-rumpus seven-year-old brother.

Oh, yeah. Cooper was going to regret this. Big-time.

3   Revenge of the Black Goo

Stuck in the Coop," Bernadette's voice oozed sympathy. "How awful is it?"

"Worse than the peat bog."

"No."

"Yes."

During their third-grade-class field trip to the Northcreek wetlands park, Calvin Kapinski had jumped on one end of the wooden bridge at the precise moment Julep had planted her foot on it. Arms whirling, she'd fallen sideways into the bog—the muddy, squishy, icky, smelly bog. Julep spent the rest of the day with the whole left side of her body covered in a thick layer of mud, which, once it dried, turned into some kind of super-bond cement that glued clothes to skin and hair to clothes. Nobody would eat lunch with her. Nobody would sit next to her on the bus. Not even Bernadette or Trig. Not that Julep blamed them. She stank like a pile of manure.

Speaking of smells . . .

"There's some goo in the corner that smells funny," Julep whispered into the phone as if somehow the goo might overhear. She drew her knees up to her chest and huddled into the tightest ball she could.

"Funny how?"

"Like Harmony's meteorites."

They both knew what that meant. Cooking was about the only thing Julep's sister didn't do well. Harmony loved making oatmeal cookies. She just didn't have the patience to wait for them to finish baking. After dropping the cookies on the baking sheet, Harmony would shove them in the oven, crank the temperature up to 500 degrees, and set the timer for three minutes. When the timer went off, Harmony would pull the cookie sheet out of the oven, wave away the smoke that rose from twelve smoldering, black blobs, and pronounce her cookies done. Of course, they didn't look much like cookies. They looked, actually, like meteorites (except Harmony's meteorites were doughy in the middle). Humans could not digest them. Even Mrs. Knudsen's schnauzer, Noodles, refused to touch the charred blobs of cookie dough. And Noodles ate everything, including dandelions, newspapers, and car rags.

Wrinkling her nose and leaning forward (but not too far forward), Julep tried to describe the gunk in the corner to her best friend. "It's black with some of kind of fuzz on it." Catching sight of the angel clock on her dresser, Julep cupped her hand over the phone to finish telling Bernadette about the scary spots on her carpet. It was 9:18—forty-eight minutes past curfew. The rule was everybody had to be off the phone by 8:30 P.M. on school nights (9:00 P.M. on Fridays and Saturdays). But this was an emergency. Bernadette Reed had been away visiting her grandparents all weekend and had missed out on every horrible thing that had happened to Julep.

Julep peered over her mattress to inspect her carpet. "Do you know what dust mites are?"

"I know what ear mites are. My kitten, Pounce, had them when we adopted her from the shelter. They're tiny bugs."

Julep recoiled. "You're telling me there are insects in my carpet?"

"We put medicine in Pounce's ears and they cleared right up. Maybe there's something you can put on your carpet."

Julep peered down at the splotchy rug. "I doubt it."

"I'll ask my mom." Bernadette's mother was a doctor.

Sighing, Julep hugged Katie to her. She was relieved her calico had survived the harrowing plunge without any visible damage, though she suspected internal injuries (the stuffing in Katie's stomach was bulging out more than usual on the right side). Naturally, Cooper had not gotten into much trouble for tossing Julep's stuff out the window. He'd pretended it was an accident and gotten the lecture from their dad on respecting other people's property and treating people the way you'd want them to treat you, etc.

Yeah, like that was ever going to happen in her lifetime.

"What are you going to wear for our school photo?" Bernadette was asking.

Julep said she didn't know. "I'd rather not open the closet door. I think something died in there."

"Knowing your brother, it probably did. Can I borrow your black velvet choker with the cameo?"

"Sure." Julep leaned over to flip up the top of her pink jewelry box—yet another one of Cooper's victims. Six months ago, her devious little brother had filled it with Froot Loops and milk. Even after dumping the cereal and airing out the pale-pink felt lining, Julep had never been able to get the ballerina to spin properly again. Now, when you lifted the lid, the little ceramic ballet dancer jerked her leg a couple of times like she had a bee up her tights, and that was it. And did her parents do anything about it? They grounded Cooper for two days and made him apologize. Big deal. A halfhearted "Sorry" wasn't going to cure her spastic ballerina. The more Julep thought about how many times Cooper had done stuff to her and gotten away with it, the angrier she got. Didn't anyone care about her things? Didn't anyone care about her feelings? No and double no.

Bernadette was still rambling. ". . . I'm glad we don't have to pose for class photos anymore. I always got stuck next to Rodney Pick-apart."

Julep corrected her. "You mean Philapart."

"I meant what I said. Have you seen what he does with his nose?"

"Somebody should tell him that it's disgusting to pick your nose . . ."

". . . and not very healthy to eat it."

They both laughed, and Julep nearly fell off her bed onto the creeping carpet. She grabbed her bedpost and hung on to keep her foot from touching the big green ink stain near her desk.

That was close.

There was a tap at the door, and Julep's dad poked his head around the corner. Immediately, she buried the phone underneath her cream fleecy blanket. But it was no use. She had been caught.

"Trig or Bernadette?" he asked.

Meekly she replied, "Bernadette."

Her dad grinned. "Five more minutes, okay?"

"Okay."

"Are you in trouble?" Bernadette asked when she came back on the line.

Julep could only stare at the empty doorway. "Amazingly not. I think they are feeling guilty about making me move into this peat bog."

"Don't worry. I'll come over next week, and we'll fix it up."

"Bring matches."

Bernadette giggled. "It can't be that bad. I'll bring my string of flamingo . . ."

Julep let out a scream.

"Okay, then. No flamingo lights."

"No, it's not that. . . ."

"What then?"

Her throat closing up, Julep could only let out a tiny chipmunk chirp.

"What's wrong?" cried Bernadette.

No response.

"Julep? *Julep?* JULEP?"

It took Julep a few seconds to find her voice. And when she did, it was barely a whisper. "You know the fuzzy black goo in the corner?"

"Uh-huh."

"I think . . . I think"—Julep swallowed hard—"it just moved."

8:44 P.M.   Mood: depressed

Dear Journal:

It's me. I mean, who else would it be? I guess it could be my sister reading you. Or my brother scribbling pictures of worms in you. But it's just boring, see-through me. There should be a support group for invisible middle children who are ignored by their families—not that my parents would remember to take me. W.D.I.E.T.? (No, I'm not going on a diet; see decoder page.)

I hope you're okay after your fall. A couple of your pages blew away, and your cover is a little warped, but it adds character. Now we both have wavy hair. Lucky you. ☹

It's official. We're in a peat bog called the Chicken Coop. I haven't been able to sleep for two days thinking about the zillions of dust mites crawling through my carpet. SO GROSS! I'm leaving the door open so the creeping carpet can leave anytime it wants to.

H.D.T.H. ?!!!!!!!!!!!
(Any more than ten exclamation points is too much, don't you think?)

M.M.C. Alert:
It was tofu/radish-balls-with-beans night. The things actually bounced off my plate. They had endive in them. What is endive anyway? Sounds like a swimming term. You know, back dive, front dive, endive!

C.Y.L.,

Julep Antoinette O'Toole,

M.M.M.M.C. (Note the new M.)

P.S.: I'm keeping the light on all night in case the black goo tries anything.

Julep's Secret Decoder Page

KEEP OUT!   SHUT THIS BOOK NOW!

W.D.I.E.T.: Why Do I Even Try? (There is no good answer to this question.)

H.D.T.H.: How Did This Happen? (another pointless question)

M.M.C.: My Mother's Cooking (She's into beans in a big way—GAS attack!)

C.Y.L.: Check You Later

M.M.M.M.C.: Miserable, misunderstood, MEAT-EATING middle child

MAY A TOFU/RADISH BALL ATTACK ANYBODY WHO READS THIS!

4 The JULEP Triangle

Cooper, don't blow bubbles in your milk. Why are you wearing two different colored socks? Julep, why is he—?"

"I don't know," Julep cut in. "I tried to get him to put on the blue ones, but . . ."

"Never mind," her mother said, exasperated. "I'll handle it."

Julep took a sip of her grape juice, but it didn't dissolve the lump growing in her stomach. Why did she always have to be the one to look after Cooper? Why was it left to her to make sure his hair was combed and his shirt wasn't inside out and his socks matched? Just because Julep was up, dressed, and at breakfast on time, her mother had gotten into the habit of expecting her to make sure Cooper did the same. Harmony always slept through her snooze alarm, so she didn't have to help out at all. She was rewarded for being lazy, while Julep got punished for being responsible. It was so NOT fair.

"Mom." Harmony glided into the kitchen, her blond hair sailing out behind her. "You gotta sign my permission slip for the school district talent show by Friday."

"Leave it on the counter, Harmony . . . in a rush . . . already late . . ."

"I didn't hear about any talent show," said Julep.

Harmony flapped her lilac-frosted eyelids. "It's for people with talent."

"Harm," their mother's voice warned from inside the refrigerator.

"Excusez-moi," her sister said lazily, plopping into the chair across from Julep.

Julep snagged the last piece of toast as Harmony's long, cherry-red fingernails reached for it. She was feeling pretty satisfied about it, too, until she remembered she had an important question to ask her sister. Today was her school-photo day. Julep delicately buttered the toast and, instead of taking a bite, held it out to Harmony.

Silver-blue eyes squinted in suspicion. "Did Cooper lick this?"

"No."

"Dropped on the floor?"

"Of course not."

"Pepper on it?"

"Don't be a goober."

"Then why . . . ?"

"Can't I be nice to my older sister for once?"

"You could." Harmony rolled her tongue around the inside of her cheek. "But you rarely are."

"Do you want it or not?"

A dozen beaded bracelets jingled down a thin wrist as Harmony took the slice of bread with a wary "Thanks."

"You're welcome."

The children watched their mother madly wipe down the kitchen counter. "Harmony, remember you have your thingy after school. . . . Coop, did you take your pill?"

Cooper looked up from stacking Froot Loops beside his cereal bowl. "Nope."

"Julep, he's already had his inhaler this morning. Could you do me a favor and—"

"Yes." Julep rolled her eyeballs into her nose as far as they could go. She got up to get Cooper's bottle of allergy pills from the drawer by the dishwasher, moving just in time as her mother flitted past her out of the kitchen. Her mother hardly ever finished a sentence when she was in her morning panic mode. Not that she ever needed to. It was always "Julep, could you . . . ?" and "Julep, will you . . . ?" and "Julep, I really need you to . . ."

Just once, Julep wished her mother would demand as much from the oldest as she did from her middle daughter. But it would never happen. Harmony, a.k.a. Miss Perfect, was the favorite. She got to lead a life of luxury.

"Here." Julep slapped a round white pill down on the table beside a stack of Froot Loops that was starting to resemble the Leaning Tower of Pisa.

Harmony was reading the newspaper and nibbling on her toast. Julep knew it was now or never. She considered never.

Never would have been the wisest choice. But she really needed this favor. Julep had decided to take a bold step. She was going to attempt to transform herself into somebody a-MAZ-ing. Somebody visible. And if she was to succeed, she would need her sister's help. Didn't it just figure?

Julep took a deep breath. "Harmony?"

"Huh?" She did not look up.

"I was wondering if maybe I could borrow—"

"No."

"You didn't let me finish."

"I didn't have to. No borrowing. No exceptions."

Harmony had tons of clothes she'd bought with her babysitting money. More clothes than she needed or knew what to do with. Some of the shirts and sweaters and skirts she'd crammed into her overstuffed closet still had tags dangling from them. Julep wasn't old enough to babysit or buy her own clothes. She'd worn the same sensible clothes her mother had picked out for her a zillion times already. All Julep wanted was to wear the softest black angora sweater on Earth for her school photo—the one with the glittering silver threads running through it. The sweater, Julep was certain, would get her noticed. She might even get a compliment from Danica Keyes, the most beautiful and popular girl in the sixth grade. It wasn't impossible. It had happened before—twice, actually, in the past six months. Last spring, not two hours after Mr. Lee had stapled Julep's poem "Butterflies" onto the class bulletin board, Danica had stopped Julep in the girls' bathroom.

"I liked your poem," she'd said, "especially the part about the white butterflies brushing their wings against the lavender." Danica's long fingers fluttered hypnotically in front of Julep's eyes. Stunned that Danica Keyes was speaking directly to her, Julep could barely stammer, "Uh . . . gee . . . thanks."

Then, on the last day of school, while everybody was racing out of class for the last time, Danica had said to Julep as they passed, "See you in middle school." Arching a dark eyebrow, she'd grinned and added, "Maybe we'll have a class together."

Okay, technically it wasn't a compliment, but it was close. After all, anyone who thinks you're slug slime isn't going to hope they get put in a class with you.

Unfortunately, in both instances, nobody had heard Danica's comments. But this time, things would be different. When Danica gushed to Julep about how much she adored her black, sparkly angora sweater, there were going to be plenty of witnesses.

Careful. Don't get ahead of yourself. You have to get the sweater first.

"Coop," Julep warned as her brother slid the pill back toward her. "Take. Drink. Swallow. Harmony," she tried again, "I don't see why—"

"You don't see why? You *don't* see why?" Dramatically, Harmony shook out the newspaper. "Would you like me to remind you about a certain floral blouse that got sliced because I trusted a certain klutzoid who crossed her heart and promised me she would guard it with her very life?"

Julep cringed. It hadn't been her fault. Not really. Julep had worn the delicate georgette blouse to help out at Bernadette's cousin's birthday party last March. She was cutting out the pin-the-tail-on-the-donkey tails and didn't realize, until it was too late, that, along with snipping out the tails, she had also cut off most of the flouncy trim on the left sleeve. She had done her best to sew the ruffle back on, but it had come out crooked, with pieces of white elastic hanging out. Harmony had gotten so mad her misty-pink blush cheeks turned scarlet red (along with her earlobes and most of her neck). It could have happened to anybody.

"It . . . it was an accident," Julep stammered, trying to wipe the picture of the flopping white elastic out of her brain.

"It's always an accident with you," said Harmony drily.

"This time, I will be really, really, really careful. . . ."

"The answer is no. Shall I spell it out for you? *N-O.* Got it?"

"*N-O,*" repeated her brother.

"Even Cooper gets it," shot Harmony, taking a swig of juice. "Simmer, will you? It's not like it matters what *you* wear."

Sinking her teeth into her tongue, Julep gulped back a wave of tears. Was it true? Was Harmony right that nothing Julep wore could make her look better? Maybe. Maybe she was. But it was worth a try, wasn't it? Couldn't her sister, at least, let her try?

"Cooper." Julep tried to keep her voice steady while her mind raced to come up with another way to convince Harmony to change her mind. "Take your pill. Now."

Carefully, he placed another Froot Loop on the top of his tower. "In a minute."

"I don't have a minute." Julep threw the bottle of pills on the table.

The quake sent Cooper's Froot Loop tower toppling. The seven-year-old sucked in his lips, dug his spoon into the cereal, and flicked a spoonful of milk at her. It splattered on her nose and cheeks, and Julep felt a dribble of sugary liquid hit her lips. Pink speckles dotted the front of her white turtleneck. "Coop!"

"Pink rain." Her brother snorted, scooping up the fallen cereal tower and tossing a handful of it into his mouth.

"Another accident?" Harmony sighed and shook out her blond hair.

Julep bolted from the kitchen, taking the stairs two at a time. In her room, she plunged face-first onto her bed. Julep wanted to cry, but she was far too angry, so, instead, she pounded the pillow with her fists as hard as she could. When at last she ran out of energy, Julep lay still for a few exhausting minutes, gasping for air.

I am going to lie here forever, and nobody will even notice I am gone.

"Julep?" Her mother was calling from downstairs. "Are you about ready? You're going to be late."

Forever lasted all of two minutes and twenty-three seconds, according to her angel clock. Groaning, Julep rolled off her bed. She flung open her dresser drawer and, without looking, reached in and pulled out the first thing she touched. It was her oatmeal, Shaker-knit, pullover sweater. Two words: *Bor. Ing.*

Julep put on the sweater and took a good, long look at herself in the mirror: the upturned nose with a tiny bump in the bridge, the place on the left side of her mouth where a dimple appeared when her dad told a good joke, the eighty-seven freckles splashed across her cheeks and nose, her completely ordinary light-brown eyes.

Before he died, her grandfather used to tell Julep that her amber eyes reminded him of a Bermuda sunset. Julep had read an article in a geography magazine for kids once about the Bermuda Triangle. It was a triangular region in the western Atlantic Ocean between the island of Bermuda, the southern coast of Florida, and Puerto Rico where weird stuff happened. Supposedly, several ships mysteriously disappeared once they entered the waters of the Bermuda Triangle. Likewise, planes vanished in the airspace above the triangle, which covered about 500,000 square miles. Although most scientists said that all of the accidents had reasonable explanations, the myth lived on. If there really was a Bermuda Triangle, Julep sure wished this sweater would vanish into it (along with her eighty-seven freckles).

Still, it warmed her to think that her eyes had reminded someone of something as lovely as an island sunset. If only her grandfather were here to say it again to her now. It might have helped boost Julep's flagging spirit. But he wasn't here. And no one else could see the sunset in her eyes.

Julep glanced down at the dreary Shaker-knit sweater. This wasn't right. She wasn't being unreasonable. Harmony was. Her sister was only refusing to let her borrow the sweater because she knew how much it meant to Julep. Harmony had mounds and mounds of sweaters and shirts. She probably wouldn't even miss it if one soft, black angora sweater with silver threads disappeared into the Julep Triangle for, say, oh, about eight hours or so.

Julep looked into the mirror.

Should I? Do I dare?

Her light-copper head nodded in agreement. It was unanimous.

Poking her head into the hallway, Julep looked to her left toward her parents' room. She looked to the right toward Harmony's room. The hallway was empty. Julep took off as fast as her tiptoes, and her courage, would take her.

A while later Julep trotted down the stairs, making sure her hunter-green wool peacoat was buttoned up as far as it would go. It pinched her neck, but she didn't undo a single button. Not yet. In the kitchen, Harmony was talking on the phone to Marielle, her best friend, about a geometry test. Julep's heart punched her in the ribs as she grabbed her lunch off the counter. She stuffed the brown bag into her red backpack on top of her candy-cane-striped T-shirt and took off for the front door. The toe of one tennis shoe had just touched the front porch when . . .

"Julep!"

Twisting her ankle, she fell sideways but managed to swing her backpack so she landed on it instead of the wooden porch.

"Are you all right?" her dad said from the doorway.

"Yeah." She grimaced, sliding off her pack onto her knees. When she put weight on her foot, a sharp zing of pain stung her ankle.

Her father was holding Cooper's hand. Her brother had one arm in his jacket.

"I'm walking with Trig," she said quickly, knowing what he was about to ask. "Can't Mom drive him?"

"She's already gone to work."

Julep got to her feet, slinging her backpack over one shoulder. "Can't you?"

"Julep, this is silly. You're both going in the same direction."

Another *small* sacrifice to ruin her life. But she could hardly argue. Only a big parking lot separated Valley View Elementary from Heatherwood Middle School, so, though Julep had graduated to middle school this year, she had still gotten stuck walking with Cooper. Why didn't her parents just Velcro the kid to her backpack and be done with it? W.A.N.

"Fine," Julep muttered, backing down the front steps when she saw Harmony pass behind her father. "But I'm leaving now."

Julep and Cooper met Trig two blocks down on the corner of Chenault and Bayview. Trig Maxwell was wearing his usual Seattle Mariners baseball cap backward. His enormous gray sweatshirt fell almost to the knees of his faded jeans. Bernadette once described Trig as looking like he'd come out of the dryer, slightly wrinkled, but comfortable. Trig blew a lime-green bubble and popped it with his teeth. "Hi, Pooper-Scooper Cooper."

Cooper opened his mouth and waggled his tongue.

"Catching flies again?" Trig snorted.

"Ribbit" came Coop's response.

"Is that what you're gonna be for Halloween?"

Cooper shook his head. "I'm going to be a big-screen TV."

"You are not." Julep turned to Trig. "He is not."

"Am so. And Julep's gonna take me out trick-or-treating," he announced.

"I am not," she gasped. Julep had already made plans to trick-or-treat with Bernadette and didn't need any irritating little brother tagging along, complaining that it was too cold or that he needed to stop and pop his blisters. When it came to collecting candy, only the strong survived. And Julep wasn't about to cut short valuable trick-or-treating time for a whimpering, whining Cooper, who still, by the way, had not said "Thanks" to her for giving up her room.

"I am definitely not taking you T.O.T.-ing," Julep said more firmly. "Harmony can take you." But even as she said the words, Julep knew it wouldn't happen. Harmony would, of course, have already made plans with Marielle. Her sister would sweet-talk her parents into letting her go out, and Invisible Girl would be forced to look after her brother yet again. She could almost hear her sister's frigid tone. "It's not as if you're popular or anything," Harmony would say. "I have to go. People are expecting *me* to be there."

"I'm not going with Harmony." Cooper's stern tone brought Julep back to reality. "She took me two years ago. She refused to go any farther than the end of our block. I got eight pieces of candy." He looked up at Trig. "You want to come with us?"

"Naw. I'm going forking."

"What's that?"

"You don't know what forking is?"

Cooper shook his head.

"I don't know, either," said Julep.

"You can't explain it," said Trig. "You have to experience it."

"Don't cross Glenwood without us," Julep yelled as her brother skipped ahead of them. "And I'm still not taking you trick-or-treating." She undid the top two buttons of her coat so she could, at last, breathe.

Trig turned to her. "What's wrong?"

"Who said anything was wrong?"

"Not me." He put up his hands to signal he wouldn't press her.

They marched down two blocks in silence before Trig said, "It's just that your face . . ."

"My face what?" she spit, not in any mood for a sarcastic remark.

"It looks . . . well, it looks like one of those burned raisins in your sister's meteorites."

That made Julep giggle. Relaxing a bit, she told him about having to swap rooms with Cooper over the weekend (she did not mention the holly-bush incident). She told him about Cooper's tantrum this morning and how he'd sprayed her with pink milk. (She did not mention the sweater incident. Some things were too personal.) When Julep finished, Trig whipped off his baseball cap, ruffled his dark-red hair, and said, "I don't get it. Why didn't you say no to trading rooms?"

"I wanted to . . . I mean, I thought about it, but . . ." Julep floundered. It wasn't easy to explain to your co-best friend who wasn't a middle child what life was like when you *were* a middle child.

Trig blew another lime bubble. "Seems like you've got no one to blame but yourself." His words echoed inside the transparent green ball.

Julep's jaw dropped. Clamping her mouth shut, she shook her head and walked a little faster. Boys could sure be irritating sometimes. Everything was always black and white with them. Yes or no. This or that. But life just wasn't that way. Life was more like a kaleidoscope, with all its faceted images and colors constantly crashing and bumping and blending into one another. Bernadette said that boys' brains developed slower than girls'. Julep didn't know if it was true or not, but it sounded possible. Particularly now.

Keeping up with her stride for stride, Trig snapped the bubble, and it fell against his face. "You want me to help you get it back?" He peeled the gum off his chin, moss-green eyes twinkling with mischief. Trig was always coming up with clever plans to scheme his way out of things. Sometimes they worked. Sometimes they didn't. On the day everybody in the fourth grade was supposed to take the state standardized tests, Trig showed up with a note from his doctor that said he had an inflamed sphygmomanometer, and he would need to be excused from stressful things like test taking. It would have worked, too, if Mrs. Newkirk hadn't checked with the school nurse and found out that a sphygmomanometer is that pumpy thing the doctor uses to take your blood pressure.

Julep did not answer.

"You're mad."

"I'm not mad," she insisted, scratching her temple.

"Are so. You're getting Follicles of Fury."

Friends who knew you better than you knew yourself could be so infuriating.

Okay, she *was* mad, but, more than anything, Julep was frustrated. Nobody understood her point of view. And how could they? Bernadette was an only child, and Trig was the baby in his family. He had a thirteen-year-old sister. Neither one of her co-best friends had ever been a middle child. Neither one of them had ever been squished beyond recognition between their siblings.

There had to be a way to get people to stop looking through her and really *see* her. But Julep didn't have any idea how to make that happen.

What should she do?

Where should she start?

How in the world do you make air appear?

Through first-period math, second-period English, and now, third-period science, Julep kept turning Trig's words over in her mind.

You have no one to blame but yourself.

Had she let this happen to her? Was it really her own fault?

Even if Julep had rejected the room swap, her parents would have certainly overruled her. Her mother had only pretended to ask Julep's opinion in the first place so as not to feel guilty. No. Trig was wrong. This mess was beyond Julep's control. She couldn't have done anything to prevent it. Besides, it was too late now. Julep might as well accept that she would be forever stuck in the dirty, smelly Chicken Coop with the creeping, dog-doo carpet.

She moved her wrist back and forth to watch the little silver threads of her sister's black sweater glitter under a shaft of sunlight. It was pretty, all right, but would it be enough? Would Danica, or anybody else for that matter, notice her for once?

A piece of paper floated down over her arm. Mrs. Lindamood was handing back their reports from last week on the water cycle. Julep was mortified to find her paper covered with so many red circles it looked as if had the chicken pox. Mrs. Lindamood's pen had found at least a dozen words—misspelled words, apparently. Others were underlined, crossed out, and punctuated with question marks to indicate her teacher's confusion about what she'd meant.

There was no grade on the page: only two words, but they were the worst words, the saddest words, the most disheartening words ever known on Earth. At the top of Julep's paper, Mrs. Lindamood had written: *See Me*.

5   Is This Thing On?

From the moment Danica Keyes glided into the cafeteria, Julep could not stop her elbows and knees from fidgeting. With her long, smooth, sable-black hair that ended in baby corkscrew curls, deep-green eyes, and soft pink lips that shimmered with clear gloss, Danica Keyes was the most beautiful and popular girl in school. Everything about Danica matched, from the top of her fourteen-karat gold barrettes to the tip of her fourteen-karat gold toe ring. Julep could not recall Danica Keyes ever wearing the same outfit twice. Once she'd overheard Danica say that she never liked to wear clothes after the newness had been washed out of them. Julep imagined herself saying that to her mother. Her mom would have laughed hysterically and made Julep fold a load of laundry to bring her back down to the planet.

Each day at lunch, Danica could be found surrounded by a group of girls, mainly Jillian Winters, Betsy Foster, and Kathleen O'Halleran and a few other sixth-grade "wannabes" who longed to be part of her royal flock but never would be. Trig had dubbed

Danica "the head goose" and nicknamed her tagalong friends "the goslings." At this very moment, the head goose and her goslings were at the end of the lunch line, buying pizza wedges and milk. When she walked, Danica's hair fluttered out behind her like a velvety black curtain (one that hadn't been flung out the window by a certain pain-in-the-rumpus seven-year-old brother).

Danica was hesitating. She was changing direction. She was turning, turning. . . .

Julep dropped her bag of organic beet chips into her lap.

Danica Keyes, the most beautiful and popular girl in the sixth grade, had chosen to honor Julep's row with her presence. She was coming this way! Today was the day that Danica was, finally, going to say something nice to Julep in front of other people.

Quickly, Julep straightened up, and her back cracked in protest.

Head up. Bright smile. Hair, look less wavy. Freckles, lighten up.
Well, do your best.
Sweater, do your stuff.

"So how did it go?" From across the table, Bernadette was popping the top off her strawberry-mango yogurt.

"Huh?" Out of the corner of her eye, Julep kept a close watch on the head goose and her goslings, who were taking their time ambling down the row. In about twenty seconds they were going to pass directly behind her. Nervously, Julep retied the little black bow at the neck of Harmony's sweater.

"I asked how your photo went."

"I . . . um . . . fine. It went fine." Julep was fluffing out her sleeves where they poofed at the shoulder.

"You'll never guess who was right ahead of me in line. Guess. Just try to guess. . . ."

"I . . . I . . . don't know." Julep could feel the flock coming closer. She retied the bow at the neck again.

"Rodney Pick-apart. Can you believe it?"

A tray clattered next to Bernadette. Trig's long legs slid into the seat beside her. "What is that guy's problem with his nose, anyway?"

"It's not." Bernadette snickered.

"It's not what?"

"No, it's *snot*," snickered Bernadette until Trig finally caught on. Inspecting him, she wrinkled her forehead. "Is that what you wore for your picture?"

Trig tugged on the front of his orange tee. "What?"

"Nothing, if you want to look like one of those flaggers on the highway."

"Works for me."

Bernadette made a face at the heap of steaming, greasy crinkle fries that covered Trig's plate. The girls watched him rip open a packet of salt and turn the mound of fries into a snow-capped volcano.

"That is soooo unhealthy, Maxwell." The reflection of the sun off Bernadette's gold wire-rim glasses stung Julep's eyes.

"I'm thinkin' those Ho Hos you got there, Reed, aren't exactly vitamin packed."

"At least I drink milk instead of sugary sodas all the time."

"I'm lactose intolerant."

"Yeah, you're intolerable, all right." Bernadette flipped her long, dark hair over one shoulder.

"I think your hearing is as bad as your eyes. I said—"

"I heard you the first time."

"You know, Reed . . ."

A slight breeze tickled the back of Julep's neck, making her shiver. Danica was right behind her! She was telling one of the goslings ahead of her to keep going. Julep slowly inhaled. Dipping her head slightly, she swung her eyes to the left to wait for the girls to reappear on the other side. Julep played with the ends of her sleeves, repeatedly pulling at the left one, which kept creeping upward. Danica was so close, Julep could smell the spearmint Life Savers she always sucked on. But where was she? Why had she stopped? There was so much noise in the cafeteria, not to mention Bernadette and Trig's endless bickering, that Julep couldn't hear what was going on behind her.

Julep would give her entire bank account, all $347.22 of it, if her friends would shut up for ten seconds. They were going to drown out Danica's compliment and ruin everything. Sometimes, it seemed Trig Maxwell and Bernadette Reed were at opposite ends of a tug-of-rope, each yanking and hauling and grunting as hard as he/she could. They were so completely different she wondered sometimes why they were friends at all. Bernadette had a quiet sense of humor, while Trig would do anything to get a laugh out of you, even if it meant getting into trouble himself, which it often did. Bernadette was always punctual and could, with her waterproof watch, tell you what time it was in China, Italy, South Africa, or anywhere else in the world. Trig, who'd never owned a watch in his life, was in no hurry to get anywhere. Bernadette was ladylike in her purple tees, decorated with little hearts or jewels, long floral skirts, and lace-trimmed socks. Trig usually wore his Mariners baseball cap (backward), a navy fleece vest, a T-shirt, and a pair of jeans—all wrinkled, even the hat. Bernadette played oboe, first chair (okay, she was the *only* chair). The best Trig could do when it came to music was get a couple of squeaks out of blowing through two sheets of toilet paper cupped in his hands. Even so, they were the two best friends she'd ever had. So if, once in a while, their personalities clashed, she supposed it was worth it. Today, however, Julep didn't feel like playing referee to their silly arguing. She had more important things on her mind.

A bead of sweat trickled down Julep's back. Why was Danica still behind her? What was going on? Had she seen the sweater? Maybe she was waiting for Julep to turn around and say something first.

Look graceful.

Look casual.

Look at all the broken purple chips in your lap.

What normal person eats beet chips anyway?

". . . so what'd you get?" Bernadette was intently gazing at her.

"Get?"

"On your water cycle assignment."

"Oh . . . I, uh . . ." She didn't want to confess to her co-best friend, who never got less than an A minus on anything, that Mrs. Lindamood was making her write it over again due to her messy writing and a few misspelled words. Okay, fourteen misspelled words.

Suddenly, there was a sharp pain in her back. With a yelp, Julep jerked around.

"Sorry, didn't see you there." Jillian clutched her flute case closer to her body while juggling a slice of pizza and can of soda pop. "Betsy, quit hogging the aisle. You made me hit Judy," Jillian said, falling into step behind Betsy, who was behind Kathleen, who was behind Danica, whose shiny black hair was waving farewell.

"My name's Julep." She turned to correct them, but nobody was listening.

That was it. It was all over. Julep's poofed-up shoulders began to sag.

Nobody had seen the sparkly sweater. Or the girl in it. After all she had endured to wear the stupid thing, it was more than a little depressing. As usual, everybody who was anybody had looked right through her. Julep was starting to wonder if there was anything worth seeing anyway.

Fishing around in her lunch bag, Julep brought out an egg-salad sandwich. It was squashed flatter than a page of notebook paper.

"Oook." Bernadette made a sour face.

Julep figured she must have smashed the sandwich when

she'd tripped on the porch that morning. Gingerly, she began unwrapping the steamrolled egg salad. Maybe she could fluff it up or something. She took a couple of bites. Actually, the compacted egg salad tasted rather good—a little warm, but good. She finished the first half of the sandwich and was about to start on the second when Bernadette shoved a piece of paper across the table. "I copied this from one of my mom's allergy books for you. It's an article about dust mites. Check out that picture." She pointed, making it impossible for Julep to tuck the article into her coat pocket. "It's blown up, like, a hundred times so you can really see what the dust mites look like. Aren't they awful?"

Forced to glimpse the big, hairy bug with eight legs, Julep quivered. "Yuck."

"They are microscopic—" Bernadette started to say, and was cut off by Trig, who jumped in with "Like your brain, right?"

She threw her Ho Ho wrapper at him.

"It says here"—Julep ran her finger down the page—"that dust mites are related to spiders. They live in sofas, carpets, blankets, and beds—anywhere we shed our skin. They feed off dead skin, and then they poop. It's the poop that causes human allergies and asthma."

"Heinous," said Trig with a grimace.

"A female can lay up to fifty eggs every three weeks." Julep glanced up in horror. "That means there could be hundreds of millions of these things crawling around in my creeping carpet right now."

"And in your bed," said Bernadette. She turned to Trig. "I've seen *your* room. There are probably billions in your pillow alone."

Pretending to ignore her, Trig asked, "So how do you kill them if you can't see them?"

"Vacuum," said Julep, reading the list of tips at the bottom of the page. "Also, it says you have to do all the other stuff my parents did, like getting mattress and pillow covers. And you have to get rid of the carpet." Julep knitted her brows. Cooper could get some pretty bad asthma attacks, but she'd had no idea that millions of these tiny creatures were to blame.

"If it were me," said Bernadette, "I couldn't even sleep in that room knowing all those insects were everywhere eating my skin and pooping."

"Somebody has to," Julep muttered, licking a bit of egg salad off her finger.

True, the mites were disgusting, but they wouldn't make *her* sick. They could really hurt Cooper, and she knew it. She had seen the effects with her own eyes. Julep folded up the article, lifted her peacoat off the bench beside her, and crammed the paper into one of the front pockets.

Suddenly, a rattling boom jolted the cafeteria. Startled, Julep dropped what little was left of her egg-salad sandwich on the table. The clap of thunder was immediately followed by the shrill *eeeeyoww* of microphone feedback. People began clamping their hands over their ears to shut out the painful noise. Julep stared at the big, black speakers, one mounted on each side of the stage. Usually, if someone was going to make an announcement about elections or a fund-raiser, the curtains would open so the person could walk onto the stage with the microphone. But the curtains weren't parting, and nobody was coming onstage.

"What's happening?" Julep shouted to Bernadette, who had her hands over her ears, too. Her co-best friend shrugged her shoulders.

Unfazed, Trig kept right on eating. Typical male.

As the sound of feedback faded away, it was replaced by a boy's voice. He was already talking, and Julep had to strain to make out what he was saying above the crackling mic.

"'. . . middle school totally scares me,'" she heard him say. "'If it's a new beginning, the way my mom says, how come I feel like the same old me?'"

Julep searched her friends' faces. The voice coming over the PA sounded oddly familiar—the words, too. Where had she heard them before? Was this a play? Trig and Bernadette looked back at her with confused expressions.

The voice continued. "'Maybe I should stop waiting for everyone else to look at me differently and start doing something to change my . . . my shoes . . . I mean, myself.'"

The Heatherwood cafeteria, usually buzzing with activity, had come to a virtual standstill. It was downright eerie. Nobody was talking, eating, moving around, or throwing away their trash. Everyone's eyes were glued to the speakers, because there was nothing to see. All they could do was listen.

"'So here are my goals for the year. Some are small, some

are big, but all of them just might change my destiny.' Ready? Uh . . . you ready, everybody?"

"Yes!" came the exuberant response from the packed cafeteria.

Trig tapped his chin. "Is that Calvin?"

An uncomfortable tingle was already traveling up the back of Julep's neck. It was beginning to dawn on her where she had heard this before. And why she had to stop it immediately. Julep popped to her feet and sprinted down the row. She could hear Bernadette calling her name, but there was no time to explain.

Calvin cleared his throat over the PA. " 'Number one goal: I want to try to make a new friend in every class I have.' "

Julep got stuck behind a group of seventh-graders who'd stopped in the middle of the aisle to hear the list. They were clogging the way. She couldn't get through.

"Excuse me, excuse me!" Julep tried to push through the logjam of bodies. "Please, move . . . get out of the way. . . ."

It was critical that Julep reach Calvin before he got to number five. He positively, absolutely could not read number five out loud.

" 'Number two: I'm going to listen more. Sometimes, I totally space and don't even hear what my friends are saying.' Uh, let's see. . . . 'Number three: Stop pigging out on chocolate. I don't have zits yet, but I'm sure they're going to explode out of my eighty-seven freckles any second now.' "

The lunchroom roared with laughter.

"Excuse ME!" Julep managed to squeeze through the pack

of seventh-graders, but she was still about twenty feet from the steps leading to the stage when Calvin rattled off number four. " 'I've got to do something about my wild hair. It's like it's from another planet or something. I . . . uh . . . can't stand my hair from Venus. W.A.N.' " He paused. "Whatever that means . . ."

Julep hurdled the steps in two bounces. However, the toe of her tennis shoe caught the top step, and she landed on her chest with a thundering *splat*. Her body hydroplaned across the freshly waxed wooden floor and cruised to a stop in the center of the stage.

". . . Uh, 'number five . . .' "

"Noooooooooo," screeched Julep, grabbing hold of the curtain to help her get to her feet. Frantic, she began slapping the red velvet curtain, trying to find the opening.

Don't say it. I'm begging you, Calvin. Not number five.

" '. . . I've got to stop daydreaming in class,' " said Calvin.

Julep was pummeling the curtain now, desperate to break through. But she was too late. In crystal-clear stereophonic sound, Calvin's mocking tone descended upon the cafeteria. " 'Last week in science I spent the whole period dreaming that Orlando Bloom stopped me at Burger King and told me I should be a model. He shared his onion rings with me. Then he kissed me. It was incredible. Of course, I totally missed the . . .' "

Calvin's voice was drowned out by an explosion of whoops and whistles.

Not that it mattered. The rest of the sentence only mentioned how she'd forgotten to take notes on the photosynthesis video.

Numb from the brain down, Julep dropped her arms. Was this real? Had Calvin Kapinski, the most obnoxious kid in the history of Heatherwood Middle School, just read a very private page out of Julep's very private journal to the entire population of first lunch?

But where had he . . . ?

How had he . . . ?

Of course! He'd snagged the page from her yard last week after her stuff had taken a header out her former bedroom window. It was the only possible explanation.

After about ten seconds of silence, Julep let out a relieved breath. Calvin was finished. At least he hadn't remembered to mention her . . .

"'C.Y.L.'" echoed off the cafeteria walls. "'Love always, Julep Antoinette O'Too'—hey, I'm not done—"

There was some rustling, then a scraping sound.

"Yes, you are. Give me that." It was Mrs. Flaskin to the rescue—if a little late. With her bad knees and orthopedic shoes, it had taken the overweight lunch monitor several minutes to nab Calvin, something he had most certainly taken into consideration when concocting his evil plan.

Click.

The microphone went dead.

It occurred to Julep that she was still standing on the stage. Her back to the crowded lunchroom, she slowly turned. Kids began to cheer and applaud. A few boys, like Eddie Levitt and Carl Stickney (Calvin's buddies), puckered up and made kissing noises.

Get out. Get out.

What are you waiting for? Get OUT!

Flying down the stairs, Julep bolted through the cafeteria doors and charged for the safety of the girls' bathroom. That was where Bernadette found her several minutes later—huddled in the corner, her head buried in her knees.

"It wasn't so bad, Julep."

Julep lifted her head, narrowing her eyes to glare at her friend.

"Come on, you gotta act like it was no big deal. That's the only way to get to Calvin." Bernadette knelt beside her. "As long as he thinks you're embarrassed, he'll keep it up. Pretend you didn't even notice, and you've got him. What can he do then?"

Julep was willing to consider that Bernadette might— MIGHT have a point. Of course, it wasn't Bernadette's personal thoughts that Calvin had shared with a couple hundred sixth-, seventh-, and eighth-graders. Still, Bernadette's logic made sense. If Julep acted like she thought the whole thing was funny, Calvin would have no reason to torment her anymore, right?

Maybe.

As Julep debated whether or not she ought to spend the rest of the day cowering in the girls' bathroom, Millie Aldridge bounded through the door. Her brown ponytail swung from side to side. "Thank goodness," she huffed, handing Julep a pink slip. "I've been looking everywhere for you."

It was a note requiring Julep's presence in the main office.

"Me?" gasped Julep. It was so not fair. Why was *she* being called to the office when the whole incident was Calvin's fault? What had Julep done wrong? Knowing Calvin Kapinski, he had already found a way to blame it on her.

"Mr. Wilcox is probably going to make Calvin say he's sorry," Bernadette said.

"Oh." Julep hadn't thought of that. "I'll skip it, thanks."

"I really think you should come," encouraged Millie.

"I don't want to see that smirk on Calvin's face," said Julep, letting the note glide to the floor.

"Calvin?" Millie wrinkled her nose. "No, it's not Calvin. It's your brother. . . ."

"Cooper?" Bernadette and Julep said together.

"He's in the nurse's office." Millie's hands flew in all directions. "You know, at the elementary school? They want you to come . . . I mean, go . . . they want you to get over there right away."

6 A Secret Pact

Hey, Coop." She stroked the pale-blond head lying on a white pillow so big it threatened to swallow him whole. "You okay?"

"Yeah . . . huh . . . I'm . . . fine." But the wheezing that sliced his words told her he wasn't fine at all. Her brother was in the middle of an asthma attack.

"Where's Miss Temple?"

"Went to . . . huh . . . call Dad again. He wasn't home . . . huh . . . the first time."

"Do you have your emergency inhaler?"

Cooper raised his left hand to show her he did.

The inhaler contained a canister of medication that helped expand the air passages in his lungs. It would relieve Cooper's wheezing and shortness of breath and restore his breathing to normal in ten or fifteen minutes. Usually.

"Is that a feather pillow?" She grabbed a section and felt for the crunch of goose down. But it was only foam. It was all right. Cooper was allergic to feathers. All of the pillows in their house were made of polyester foam.

"Sit up," Julep instructed, turning his legs so they hung down off the cot. She lowered herself beside him and began to gently pound his back with her fist to clear some of the mucus from his lungs. It was something their parents did when Coop had an asthma attack, and Julep had done it on occasion, too, when her mom or dad's hands had gotten tired.

"Feels . . . huh . . . good." Cooper's voice pulsated in time to her hits.

"What do you think happened?"

"Don't . . . know . . ."

Her brother was allergic to so many things—dust, mold, grass, weeds, most any animal with fur or feathers, wheat, peanuts, eggs—there was a whole list of stuff. Anything could have sparked his attack, from running in the chilly air at recess to getting too close to the janitor's vacuum cleaner.

Cooper used to get asthma attacks about once a week until he started taking allergy pills and using his preventive inhaler each morning. He also got injections every two weeks to help with his allergies. Now he only got a mild attack about once a month or so. When that happened, his emergency inhaler, which contained fast-acting medication, usually brought the symptoms under control. However, once every four or five months, Cooper would get a more serious asthma attack that would require his parents to take him to the doctor or hospital emergency room.

"You're gonna be all right." Julep used the strongest big-sister voice she had. "How many puffs have you had?"

He held up two fingers. In an emergency, he was supposed to take three puffs, spaced at about two minutes apart.

"Has it been a couple of minutes?" When he nodded, she said, "Let's do one more. Take your time," she reminded. Cooper had a tendency to panic and try to gulp his medication, rather than breathing in slowly. Not that she blamed him. If Julep couldn't catch her breath, it would freak her out, too.

Cooper put his lips around the spacer tube, a long mouthpiece attached to the L-shaped inhaler. The tube was designed to keep the device a few inches away from his mouth so that Cooper sucked in the medication rather than the propellant used to push it from the canister.

Her brother took a breath and pressed down on the top of the inhaler to release the medication.

"Hold it," prompted Julep. "One, two, three, four . . ."

When she reached ten, Cooper took a breath.

"Perfect," she praised. "Now just relax. You're all tight and tense."

"Easy for . . . huh . . . you to say." Two blue eyes, filled with fear, looked up at her. "How can . . . I . . . huh . . . relax?"

"Because it's all smooth sailing from here. You've had your inhaler. . . ."

"Yeah."

"And you got your shot last weekend."

"Yeah." He was starting to look more confident.

". . . And you took your pill this morning." She paused, waiting for him to acknowledge that, too. However, her brother glanced down at his swinging tennis shoes and remained silent.

"Coop?"

"Uh-huh?" His voice was thinner than a mosquito's wing.

"You *did* take your pill this morning. . . ."

No answer.

"Cooper?"

His chin fell forward onto his chest. "I was . . . huh . . . makin' the world's . . . huh . . . tallest Froot Loop tower."

"Cooper Maynard O'Toole," she scolded. "You can't forget your pill. You've got to take it every day. *Every* day. I can't be responsible for you all the time. You're not a baby anymore."

A tear slipped down a splotchy-red cheek. "I know, but—"

"Okay, okay," she said quickly, realizing that upsetting him would only make things worse. It was crucial that Cooper remain calm so he would take the slow, even breaths necessary to help subdue the attack. "I didn't mean to yell," Julep said apologetically. "Let's flip you, okay?" She leaned her brother over her knees so she could pound his back a little harder.

"Ju-ells?" He said her name in rhythm to the hits.

"Uh-huh."

He tugged on the ribbed edge of her sweater. "Isn't this . . . huh . . . Harmony's?"

"Uh . . . I, uh . . ."

Before she could stammer out an answer, Miss Temple

came back into the room. "All righty, your dad is on the way. How are we doing?"

"Okay," Cooper said, his breath still raspy.

Julep helped him sit up straight so Miss Temple could take his pulse and blood pressure.

"You are breathing much better," she said. "I think the meds are kickin' in, kiddo. Can you drink some juice for me?"

Cooper said he could.

"First, go rinse out your mouth," the nurse instructed. "There are cups in the bathroom." They all knew it was important for Cooper to wash out his mouth after using his inhaler to keep from getting hoarse.

"Thanks for coming," Miss Temple whispered to Julep while Cooper was in the bathroom. "He kept asking for you and wouldn't settle down until I sent for you. Sorry to have to take you out of class."

Julep gave her a shy grin. "I was at lunch. I didn't mind. Really."

Miss Temple had *no* idea.

The nurse popped the spacer tube off the inhaler and washed it out with soap and water. She dried it and placed it, along with the inhaler, in a white plastic box with Cooper's name on it. Opening the refrigerator, Miss Temple took out a plastic jug of apple juice and filled a Dixie cup about half-full.

"Sip that, kiddo." The nurse handed Cooper his juice when he came out of the bathroom. "I've got another patient to check on, but I'll be right around the corner if you need me."

After a few more minutes, once Julep was sure that Cooper's asthma was improving, she said, "I'd better go. If I miss stretches in PE, The Borg will—"

"Stay." He grabbed for her sleeve and nearly spilled juice all over both of them.

"Careful," Julep said, stepping out of the way as a sprinkle of yellow liquid showered her tennis shoes. "Harmony will kill me if I get anything on this."

"I knew it was . . . huh . . . her sweater."

Julep gave him a pleading look. "You won't tell, will you?"

He cocked an eyebrow. "Depends."

"On what?" she asked cautiously.

"You gonna take me trick-or-treating?"

"Cooper Maynard O'Toole." She folded her arms. "That is completely unfair."

Her brother grinned broadly and shrugged as if to say, "Seems fair to me."

Julep put her hands on her hips. She paced the room. She lightly pounded her fist against the wall. And Cooper watched it all with a sly grin. He knew he'd won. And she knew it, too. What could she do? It was either give in to Cooper's demands or deal with one seriously crazed sister, and all of the painful consequences that went with it, when she got home. Julep only hoped that Bernadette wouldn't be too upset when she found out they were going to have to take Cooper trick-or-treating with them.

"Okay,"—Julep surrendered—"but there are a few conditions."

"Conditions?"

"Yes."

"Like what?" Cooper frowned suspiciously. He thought she was trying to trick him. Hardly. She, however, was merely trying to survive.

"Raise your right hand. That's your left."

"Sorry." He switched the cup from his right hand to his left.

"Repeat after me. I will not tell Harmony that Julep borrowed her sweater."

"Repeat after me."

"Very funny."

Cooper chuckled. "I will not tell Harmony that Julep borrowed . . . huh . . . her sweater." He rolled his eyes when he said "borrowed" to indicate they both knew it was the wrong verb for the crime.

"Even if I am tortured with needles in my eyes or hung upside down by my toenails . . ."

"Gross . . ."

"Say it."

"Even if I am tortured with needles . . . huh . . . in my eyes or hung upside down by my toenails . . ."

"I will not flick milk on Julep . . ."

"I will not . . ."

"I wasn't finished."

"Go ahead."

"I will not flick milk on Julep, pour a whole box of Cheerios into her backpack, or drop my Hot Wheels into her orange juice for the rest of eternity."

"Aw, come on, Jules. . . ."

Julep drew her lips into a tight line.

Reluctantly, Cooper repeated the sentence, with a few pauses to inhale fresh air. "Happy now?"

"Turn around."

"What for?"

"I need to make sure you don't have fingers, toes, or anything else crossed."

Cooper groaned, but he twirled. Julep didn't see anything crossed, including his eyes. He had tried that one on her once before. They locked pinkies to seal the deal.

"Remember you swore," she reminded him. "That means you can't say anything to Harmony about *this*." She tugged at the bow on her sweater.

"I won't."

"'Cause you have a hard time keeping secrets, Coop."

"I do not."

"Do so."

"Do not!"

"Okay, fine." She didn't want to get his asthma going again. "You don't."

"What did you get on it?" Cooper asked, pointing to her chest.

Glancing down, Julep quickly brushed off the bits of dirt and dust clinging to the front of the black angora sweater—a souvenir from her recent bodysurf across a certain cafeteria stage.

Miss Temple appeared in the doorway. "Cooper, your dad's here."

"Don't forget your coat." Julep handed her brother his jacket. "Zip up," she called as he left, knowing even as she said it that her brother would forget.

Julep let her thumb slowly slide over the poofy sleeve of her sister's sweater.

Cooper was always forgetting important stuff. And, frankly, that had her more than a little worried.

7 JUMPING JULEP

Julep skidded into the Heatherwood gym, still out of breath from getting into her PE shorts and tee at warp speed. She was eight minutes late. The class had already done its cardio warm-up and was sprawled out on the floor stretching. Julep could feel twenty-seven pairs of eyes on her as she hurried to where her PE teacher was leaning against the bleachers. Mrs. Springborg, a.k.a. The Borg (as in *Star Trek: The Next Generation* "resistance-is-futile" Borg), inspected Julep's pass like it was glowing rock from Neptune or something. The way those owl eyes stared at her without blinking always made Julep feel like she'd done something wrong, even when she hadn't.

"Acceptable," barked The Borg. "Find a spot and warm up."

Julep caught sight of Trig and Bernadette in the back line of kids by the windows. It was the only class all three of them had together, and Julep looked forward to it each day. Julep hurried to join her friends, taking the last spot in the row beside Bernadette.

"How's Cooper?" Bernadette reached out over her knees to grab her toes.

"He went home. But he'll be all right."

"What?" Trig, who was on the other side of Bernadette, couldn't hear, so she had to repeat everything Julep said to him.

Mrs. Springborg blew her whistle, and everyone flung their legs to the side so they all looked like human Vs. Bernadette leaned all the way forward, touching her nose to the ground. Just watching her do it made Julep's crotch hurt. She tried to copy Bernadette, but her nose never got anywhere near the floor. When The Borg called "Right," the class shifted to stretch over their right legs. Bernadette grabbed the sole of her tennis shoe and bent to touch her chin to the floor. Julep wiggled her fingers and leaned forward, but the best she could do was grab her upper shin.

"Very nice, Miss Reed." The Borg passed behind them. "Keep working on it, Miss O'Toole," she said, disappointment dripping from every syllable.

Julep waited until The Borg had gone to the next row to ask Bernadette, "Do you mind if Cooper goes T.O.T-ing with us?"

Bernadette groaned. "He's so slow. If we went by ourselves, we could go farther and stay out later. We could get more stuff."

"I know, but you should have seen him lying in the nurse's office gasping for breath," said Julep. "How could I say no when he asked me to take him?"

"You couldn't" came the response from underneath a curtain of dark-brown hair. "Okay, he can come."

"You're the best."

"What did she say after you said Cooper could go trick-or-treating with you guys?" Trig was asking.

Bernadette swung her head his way. "She said I was the best. You want to make something of it?"

"Not in this position," moaned Trig, who, from the looks of things, was even worse at stretching than Julep.

When they had finished, The Borg instructed each person to get a jump rope from the pile in the equipment box. The ropes were the plastic kind, with alternating blue and white beads resembling straightened macaroni noodles. Julep stood on her rope, pulling the plastic blue handles straight up toward her shoulders. The Borg said that if the ends of the rope came up to your armpits, it meant it was the right size for you. Julep's ends came up to her waist.

"Yours is too short," said Bernadette, putting her hair back into a high ponytail.

"You think?" mocked Julep. Bernadette was an expert in stating the obvious, which could be frustrating sometimes.

When Julep went back to exchange her rope, there were only two left in the box. One had no handles, and the other had several broken sections. The music was already starting. The Beach Boys were singing "Surfin' U.S.A."

"No dawdling." Mrs. Springborg's owl eyes were boring into her skull. Julep decided to keep her original rope and rushed back into place. She tried to skip, but it was so short she had to bend forward to keep from slapping the back of her head on the beads. Then she had to lift her knees up to her chin just to jump over the thing. Julep could only manage one or two jumps before the rope would whap against her head or knees or ankles.

Meanwhile, Bernadette was skipping away without missing a beat. Trig was doing pretty well, too, considering he looked about as thrilled as a sick turtle. The Borg had a silly name for each jumping exercise. There was The Flying Squirrel, where you jumped with your legs spread apart, then came back to the center like the lower half of a jumping jack. There was The Funky Frog, where you hopped on one foot. When Julep tried, she made it five times around, but on the sixth time, she caught an ankle on the skimpy rope and went down face-first. Her chin hit the wooden floor with a loud *thud*. Her teeth sank straight into her tongue. Was that blood she tasted?

"Pick it up," shouted The Borg in her direction as Julep dragged herself off the floor.

By the time the whistle blew, the bones in Julep's knees felt like they were about to crumble. A cramp was slicing through her calf. Her tongue was starting to swell.

"It's over," gasped Julep, dropping her rope.

"It's not over," called The Borg. "We're going to finish with a contest. When you hear the music, everyone begin jumping. The first time you miss, you must sit down. The last person still standing—I mean jumping—wins the contest."

Danica waved her hand. Her silky hair was divided into two pigtails and tied with matching pink ribbons. Julep noticed that Betsy and Kathleen, who were standing near her, also had their hair in pigtails and tied with pink ribbons.

"Mrs. Springborg?" asked Danica. "Can we jump any way we want?"

The Borg said they could and told them to get ready.

Julep could feel welts rising on her legs. Her tongue hurt. Her calf ached. She had a plan. She would jump once, miss, then quickly drop to the floor to rest her aching, bruised body. It was what everyone would expect her to do, and besides, she needed the rest. The Borg started the music. This time it was Britney Spears singing "Oops! . . . I Did It Again." Julep swung the rope over her head, barely lifting her feet. She waited for the plastic beads to swat her ankles, but instead, the rope slid under her toes. So she jumped once more. Then again. And again.

"I think I've got the hang of this." She scrunched her shoulders as the rope came around for the tenth (or was it the eleventh?) time.

"Go, Julep!" Bernadette cried, easily leaping over her rope.

Although she was leaning forward, her knees nearly banging her chin with each skip, Julep did not make a mistake. She could hear kids around her collapsing to the floor. Turning her head slightly, she saw that Trig had already missed and was down. Julep wanted desperately to stop, too. Her thighs screamed in pain. The plastic handles were cutting into her hands. She knew she must look ridiculous.

Just quit. There's not even a prize for winning. Just stop, why don't you? STOP!

Her mind kept giving her perfectly good reasons to give up, but her feet didn't seem to be paying any attention. As if on automatic pilot, they kept right on leaping over the beaded rope.

Bernadette squealed. She had gotten caught up in her rope. Seeing her friend drop to the floor, Julep was a millisecond away from giving up when The Borg yelled, "Nice jumping, Miss O'Toole."

With those words from her teacher, Julep felt a surge of strength zap her body. Julep's shoulders perked up. Her toes felt invigorated. Her brain blocked out all sensations of pain.

Soon, a soft chant began to rise from the back row.

"Go, Julep. Go, Julep. Go, Julep. . . ." It was Bernadette, Trig, Millie, Rodney, and some of the others who had also missed and were down.

"Getting . . . tired . . ." she panted, feeling a strange tug at her left side.

"You can do it," Bernadette shrieked. "It's just Betsy, Danica, Calvin, and you left. Come on, Julep, you can win this thing. . . ."

Win? WIN? Julep had never won anything in her life (as her sister so frequently pointed out). More than anything, she wanted to beat Calvin, to show him that he couldn't humiliate her and get away with it. Julep needed to find a way to erase what had happened to her during lunch—and this was it!

Sweat dribbling down her back, Julep was beginning to think that maybe she *could* win. All she had to do was hold on a little longer . . . just a little longer. . . .

A sharp pain stabbed Julep in the side, but she refused to think about it.

Keep going. Keep going. Think about something else.

A field of daisies.

Persian kittens.

Corn dogs.

Strike that. No corn dogs. No food.

"Betsy's down," Trig hooted.

"It's down to Danica, Calvin, and you." Bernadette was bouncing up on her knees.

"Go, Julep. Go, Julep. Go, Julep. . . ."

The chant whirled around her head. Across the gym, she could hear the goslings cheering for Danica, but Julep focused only on those calling her name. "Go, Julep. Go, Julep. . . ."

Julep's legs felt as if they were lime Jell-O melting in the August sun. But she wasn't about to give up. Not when she was so close to finally doing something right, something completely un-Julep.

"Calvin dropped out," called Trig. "Jump, Julep! *Jump!*"

"I . . . am. . . ." she gasped, ducking as she flung the rope overhead.

If you do this, you'll be a hero. Imagine it—people coming from across America (and Europe) to Snohomish, Washington, to watch the spectacular, superhuman Jumping Julep Machine. She never misses. Never! You'll compete internationally (with a rope of the correct size, of course) and take home first prize at the World Jump Roping Championships. Naturally, you'll qualify for the Olympics, where you'll Flying Squirrel your way to a gold medal with the highest point total ever in the history of rope jumping. Perfect 10s. As you bask in your glory, Nike will offer you a million-dollar contract to be the spokesman for their new line of Jumping Julep shoes (you'll get yours free). Your family will appear on the Today show and gush to Katie Couric about how fabulous you are. Danica will announce to the whole school that she likes you and beg you to sit with her and the goslings at lunch. But you'll have to say no, because your fans need you. And besides, you have a date with Orlando Bloom at Burger King. Onion rings await.

You cannot lose. You will not lose. Your future is twirling in your hands.

Get set for greatness.

The toe of Julep's shoe caught one of the beads on the rope. A gasp went up from the chanters. Julep lifted her foot, and the rope cleared without her having to take an extra step. When she made it, her fans let up a relieved "Aaaaaahhhh."

"Danica's getting tired."

"You can do it!"

Bernadette and Trig were shouting above the music.

"You've got it, Julep," whooped Trig. "You're going to win!"

"I'm . . . gonna . . . win?" As the cramp tightened its hold on her side, she wondered if making kids eat lunch right before PE class was such a good idea. "Let's get this over B.I.P." She almost stumbled when the rope grazed her shoulder.

"B.I.P.?" a puzzled Bernadette asked.

"Before . . . I . . . puke."

"You're not gonna . . ."

It was a sentence Bernadette would never get to finish.

Julep's feet may have wanted to keep going, but her stomach had other ideas.

When Julep's lunch made an appearance on the gym floor, the chanting came to an abrupt halt. So did the music. Nobody said a word. Not even The Borg, whose whistle appeared to be frozen to her lips. It was as if aliens had landed smack in the middle of the Heatherwood gym. But it wasn't aliens. It was egg salad. And it was everywhere.

After a long silence, a voice peeped from the far corner, "So does this mean I won?"

No one answered. Danica let her rope clatter to the floor.

Trig mumbled something about getting the janitor, while Bernadette put an arm around one red-faced, dizzy, out-of-breath, bent-over Julep. "Come on, Julep, let's go to the bathroom."

With her friend's arm limply draped over her shoulders, Julep felt her knees wobble as she shuffled to the locker room.

"I lost." Julep fell against the cool tiles of the bathroom stall.

"But you were close."

Julep was always close. Yet the nearer she came to victory, the worse it felt when it was ripped away from her. Julep clutched her stomach, which was still sloshing, and muttered, "I hate egg salad."

Bernadette patted her back and sighed. "We all do."

8 Misery and Monsters

Someone was tapping on her bedroom door. Holding the damp washcloth to her forehead, Julep turned her head toward the grungy green wall so whoever it was would think she was asleep. She didn't feel like being teased by Harmony or tormented by Cooper right now. Maybe, if she was lucky, the creeping carpet would eat her for dinner, and she would never have to go to school again. But then again, she was rarely ever lucky.

"How's my Mint Julep?" her dad asked softly, entering the room.

"Sore."

"I've got some ice for your . . . your . . . where does it hurt?"

"Pick a spot." She motioned toward her legs, though her chin and head were aching, too.

He put the ice pack over the welts on her right shin and went to the bathroom to re-soak her washcloth in cold water.

"How's Cooper?" she asked when he came back.

"Healthy enough to be driving your mom crazy. How are *you*?"

"Terrific," Julep said flatly. When her father placed the cool cloth back on her forehead, Julep felt the sting of tears well up behind her eyes. "Terrible," she confessed in a whisper.

How was she supposed to face everyone at school tomorrow? It would be like the peat-bog episode all over again, but much worse. No one would want to talk to her or sit by her or, especially, eat lunch with her. Once word of this got around school, Trig and Bernadette would decide they'd had enough. They would be forced to turn their backs on her. After all, how could they risk being associated with someone so hopelessly jinxed? Even they had their standards.

"Sorry." Trig would rub the top of his dark-red hair the way he always did when he was uncomfortable. "I can't have people knowing I know you. I'll never get on the basketball team."

Bernadette would let out a sympathetic sigh. "I wish I could eat with you, Julep, but I've got my future to think about. I mean, someday I'll have to apply for college scholarships."

Julep would be an outcast—the one stuck in the back corner of class with the rickety desk that was missing its seat screws, the one assigned a locker next to the custodian's supply room in the ant-ridden basement, the one forced to eat lunch alone in the moldy white plastic chair that the cooks used to prop open the back door to the cafeteria. Up until now, the only thing that had kept her going was the knowledge that she was, at least, visible to her friends. But with that gone, what was the point of trying? What was the point of anything?

Julep felt a teardrop slide down her cheek and rolled her eyes upward, blinking rapidly. Her grandmother had told her that if you did that, you could keep yourself from crying. Julep had tried it a few times before. Once when she had fallen off the swings in third grade and once when George McMartin had made fun of the blue ceramic chicken she'd made in pottery class. Both times she had tried the trick. And it had worked.

"You know, Julep"—her dad sat down on the edge of her bed—"embarrassing things happen to everyone."

"Mostly they happen to me." Julep kept blinking until she felt sure she wasn't going to cry.

Her father stroked her hair for a few minutes. Then he said quietly, "When I was in middle school—well, they called it junior high back in the dark ages. Anyway, I played on the junior-varsity basketball team, and there was this . . . well, there was this one game. . . . see, we were playing our crosstown rivals, the Centennial Patriots. They were the best team in the city, always won the championship every year, and we were just so-so. But I was certain we could beat them because, after all, I was the star player." He grinned sheepishly, his light-brown eyes crinkling. "The night of the game the gym was packed. There wasn't a seat anywhere. And we played like we'd never played before. We were passing and dribbling the ball like pros and hitting shots we hardly ever made, even in practice. Well, we were tied with thirty seconds left in the game. Chuck tossed the ball to me, and we hustled down the court, passing the thing between us. I saw an open lane and dodged through two defenders, spun left, then right, and I let that baby fly." Her dad shot an imaginary ball toward her closet, his eyes following the invisible arc.

Julep pushed the washcloth aside. "What happened?"

"It swiveled around the rim a couple of times and, just when I was certain it was going to fall out, it went through the net. Swish!"

Julep's heart sank. "What was so awful about that?"

"After my miracle shot, I noticed the crowd wasn't going wild. My team wasn't lifting me on their shoulders or cheering or anything. However, the Patriots *were* going nuts, slapping me on the back, and celebrating. That's when I realized I'd been so busy showing off my fancy footwork I hadn't realized that somehow, I'd gotten turned around on the court. I had scored for the other team."

"Oh, no!"

He shook his head. "It was awful. Everybody at school heard about it. For a couple of weeks, I was known as Wrong Way O'Toole. They even did a little article in the town newspaper. But, after a few months, it was old news. Trust me, Julep, it may hurt today, but it will get better. Time passes, and people forget. It won't be long before you'll be able to look back on everything that happened today and laugh."

Julep wasn't so sure. Winning a game for the other team was one thing. Tossing your cookies or, in this case, your egg salad in gym was in a class by itself. She knew her dad was trying to lift her spirits, but it wasn't working. Nobody was going to forget what Julep had done. And, for sure, she was never going to be able to laugh about it. Another tear got past her defenses and slipped down her temple onto the pillow.

"I don't suppose you could homeschool me?" she asked.

Her dad thought she was joking and smiled. He slid his fingers through the hair around her ears. "Close your eyes."

Her window was open slightly to let in some fresh air, and Julep could hear frogs burping as she drifted into the foggy sapphire-blue world between reality and dreams. The Chicken Coop faced the backyard, so Julep could hear the frogs down at the pond behind their house much better here than from her old room, which looked out over the side yard and the street. Julep loved hearing the male frogs sing out to attract mates. It sounded as if they were calling *"Brr-roke, brr-roke, brr-roke."* In the springtime, you could hear them a good half-mile from the pond as hundreds of boy frogs tried to outcroak one another to compete for the females. Nobody was in sync, but it didn't matter. As summer turned to fall, and fewer and fewer frogs needed mates, the *Brr-oke* song slowly faded away. Julep was glad that a few determined frogs had hung around to serenade her now.

"Life can bring good surprises, too, you know," she heard her father say.

"Good surprises?" Her own voice sounded far away. "What kind of good surprises?"

"You'll see," he whispered.

Brr-roke, brr-roke, brr-roke.

The warbling lullaby enveloped her.

I want to be more than I am, thought Julep. *I want to be more than air.*

It was more than a wish. More than a dream. It was a prayer.

But was anybody listening?

Blueberry syrup dribbled down the sides of a stack of golden buttermilk pancakes, mingling with a swirl of melting butter. The pile of pancakes reached so high they disappeared into a lemonade sky of puffy white clouds. Julep dug her fork into the warm, squishy bread and brought it to her mouth.

"Julep? *Julep* . . ."

The pancake tower dissolved.

"You awake?"

"No." Her mouth felt like it was stuffed with a million cotton balls. She blinked against a bright tunnel of light, shading her eyes with her hand. "Cooper? What's wrong? Are you having an asthma attack?"

He clutched his brown bunny, Fred, to his chest. "Something's in my closet."

Not this again. Ever since her brother had seen the movie *Monsters, Inc.,* Cooper was convinced big, furry monsters who were a lot less friendly than Billy Crystal and John Goodman lived in his closet, too. She had tried explaining that the movie wasn't real. But Cooper was certain that his closet housed horrific beings from other worlds, and no amount of discussion was going to change his seven-year-old mind.

"Jules." He shook her shoulder. "You gotta check."

"Coop," she said with a yawn, "aren't you ever gonna outgrow this?"

He held the flashlight under his chin, the beam casting creepy shadows on his face. "I think my room is haunted."

"It was my room before it was your room, and I'm telling you it's not haunted." She pulled the blanket up over her head. After counting to twenty, she said, "You're not gone, are you?"

"No."

Julep tossed her comforter aside and got up. Irritated and sleepy, she forgot to jump over the stain blobs on the creeping carpet. Julep tramped down to the end of the hall to her old room. She slid the closet door open. She slid the closet door shut and headed back to the Coop.

"Nothing there." She collapsed into bed and yanked the blanket up to her ears. A few minutes later: "Are you still here?"

"Yup."

"You're not leaving, are you?"

"Nope."

Julep groaned. "How come when this was your room, you were sure there was a monster in *this* closet?"

"There was. It must have moved with me. Monsters have suitcases, you know, just like everybody else."

"Come on." She opened up the covers for him to climb in. It was easier to give in than keep arguing with logic like that. "There are conditions for sleeping here, you know."

"Again?"

She chose to ignore his whiny tone. "You have to promise not to hog the bed."

"I promise."

"No snoring."

"I promise."

"No kicking."

"Okay."

"Coop?"

"I said okay."

"No, not that."

"Then what?"

"Do you ever miss this room?"

"Do you miss yours?"

Constantly is what popped into her mind.

"I asked you first" is what she said.

"No," he said after a few seconds. "Why should I? It's only a room."

"Yeah," she said thoughtfully. They *were* just rooms. Of course, that was easy to say when you got to live in a glorious golden palace, instead of a cave with mucus walls and a pulsating carpet. It was SO not . . .

"Jules?"

"What?" She snapped.

"You can visit your old room any time you want."

Translation: thanks for the room.

"'Night, Jules."

"'Night, Coop."

4:28 P.M.   Mood: hopeless

Dear Journal:

We are doing outlines in English class. Here goes:

I) Julep throws up on the gym floor—I.M.L.F.?

    a. Bernadette says nobody noticed E.S. incident (very unconvincing).

    b. Trig agrees; however, his left eye won't stop twitching.

II) Julep gets several FABULOUS new nicknames:

    a. Ralph

    b. Up Chuck

    c. O'hurling O'Toole

    d. Barf-o-matic

    e. Julep Spew-Up (M.P.F.)

III) Robbie Cornfeld, who reads the morning announcements over the PA first period, says the lunch menu like this:

"Today, the cafeteria will be serving chili con carne, twisty bread, baked beans, peach cups, and apple crisp with whipped cream. There will be no egg salad. I repeat, NO egg salad."

IV) Whole class applauds. S.I.T.A.B.?

V) Calvin Kapinski follows Julep through the halls after second, third, and fourth period with a Hefty bag, just in case she has to—and I quote—"fling some chunks."

VI) Julep moves to the Bermuda Triangle, where they have probably never heard of egg salad. And if they have, it has most likely mysteriously disappeared.

VII) Gotta pack.

C.Y.L.

      Love,

      Julep, M.M.M.M.M.C.

    P.S. I hope the Bermuda Triangle is bigger than this.

Julep's Secret Decoder Page

STEP AWAY FROM THE JOURNAL AND NO ONE GETS HURT!

I.M.L.F.: Isn't My Life Fun? (Note the sarcasm.)

E.S.: Egg Salad (of course)

M.P.F.: My Personal Favorite

S.I.T.A.B.: Should I Take a Bow? (Insert more sarcasm here.)

M.M.M.M.M.C.: Miserable, Misunderstood, Meat-eating, Mysteriously-vanishing Middle Child

READ THIS AND YOU'LL GROW
BIG, HAIRY NOSE WARTS

9 Life's Little Surprises (Part I)

Ahh," shrieked Julep, banging her fist against the locker.

She'd spun her combination four times, and still the door refused to budge. There was no figuring out this thing. Half the time it opened, and half the time it didn't. Julep had tried all of the usual magic words . . .

Abracadabra.

Open sesame.

Along with a few of her own threats . . .

Unlock now, or I'll kick the stuffing out of you.

My dad has a blowtorch, you know.

But nothing was working.

Maybe Mr. Wyatt wouldn't mind if she didn't bring her math book this once. In her mind, Julep could already see his piercing glare and the way his two eyebrows converged to create a single bushy eyebrow whenever he got annoyed. And he was certainly going to be annoyed if she didn't show up to class with her book. Determined not to have the deadly unibrow aimed at her this morning, Julep set her lips tight. She was about to take one final crack at the locker when a hand brushed hers aside. "What's your combination?"

Julep's nostrils were overpowered by the scent of spearmint Life Savers, while her brain was overwhelmed by the sight of the girl standing next to her. "Uh . . . I . . . uh . . ."

"Come on. We don't have much time. The tardy bell is going to ring."

"Uh . . . twenty-two, seventeen . . . um . . ." Her mind had gone blank. ". . . Ten."

Danica Keyes twirled the knob several times to clear the lock. Julep had never before stood this close to the most beautiful and popular girl in the sixth grade. A fourteen-karat gold teardrop dangled from a petite earlobe, twinkling in the glow of the fluorescent lights. Julep wondered if it would be rude to ask Danica how she got her onyx hair to curl that way just at the very tips. She decided it would be.

"I meant to tell you." Danica was carefully lining up the twenty-two with the mark on the lock, her deep-green eyes intent on the task. "I felt really bad about all that stuff that happened to you, you know?"

Julep felt a warmth rush up her neck. Was Danica referring to the journal fiasco or the egg-salad fiasco? Or both? Not that it mattered. She would accept sympathy wherever she could get it.

"I got sick at Girl Scout camp last year." Danica sighed. "Undercooked chicken. It wasn't pretty; that's all I can say."

"I'm never eating egg salad again in my lifetime," vowed Julep.

Danica nodded to indicate it was unlikely anyone in their PE class would be eating egg salad ever again.

Julep glanced around to see if anybody was taking note that the head goose was talking to an ordinary duck, but because the tardy bell for first period was about to ring, there were only a few older girls at the far end of the hall. The eighth-graders rounded the corner and disappeared from view, leaving Julep and Danica alone in the hall. How unlucky could Julep be? She was beginning to wonder if Danica was deliberately waiting until nobody was around to talk to her.

"Calvin is such a jerk." Danica bit her lip as she delicately eased the seventeen into place. "I can't believe he read your journal out loud. You should sue him."

Could she do that?

"Could I do that?"

"After what he put you through, you could probably get a bunch of money for your pain and suffering. I know because my dad's an attorney."

Julep pondered that. "I could sue Calvin for public humiliation."

"Absolutely," agreed Danica. "But honestly"—she paused, her eyes meeting Julep's—"it wasn't so bad. In fact, I thought your list was kind of . . . sweet."

Sweet? Really? Julep had to shake her head to make sure she wasn't daydreaming.

"I thought it was great how you'd set some goals for yourself." Danica kept going. "The way you wanted to make new friends and also be a better friend. More people should do that. Plus, you write funny. I mean, you have a funny way of writing."

"Huh?" was all Julep could muster in response to something so unexpected.

She wished she had a camera to take a picture of this moment because Bernadette was never going to believe her! Danica had stopped to help Julep open her locker and compliment her writing. And the incredible thing was that Julep wasn't even wearing anything remotely fashionable—just her rust-colored Henley shirt with the missing third button and a pair of faded jeans.

"Can I ask you something?" Seeing Julep's eager nod, Danica rushed on. "You don't have to tell me if you don't want to, but what does C.Y.L. mean?"

"Oh, that." Embarrassed, Julep glanced down and stubbed her toe into the floor. "It's nothing. . . . It's part of a code I made up. . . . It's no big thing. . . . I started it after my brother got into my journal. It means Check You Later, you know, like good-bye or see you, that's all."

"Here we go." Danica raised her eyebrows as she gently scooted the ten under the arrow. Julep awaited the miracle that was sure to come. Lilac fingernails grabbed the handle and tried to lift it up. It didn't budge.

"It's not your fault," Julep was quick to say. "It's very stubborn. . . ."

Danica put more pressure on the handle. "Come on," she grunted. "Come on, you stupid thing. . . ."

This was too cool. The most popular girl in the sixth grade was yelling at and wrestling with Invisible Girl's locker. But nobody was around to see it. Julep wanted to scream so everyone would run into the hall and witness this amazing event for themselves.

With one big tug (and an even bigger grunt), Danica inched the handle upward enough to allow her to swing open the door. Had Julep not thrust out her arm, a stack of books and notebooks would have come crashing down on Danica perfect head.

"Sorry," gulped Julep. "I should clean it out."

As she caught sight of the five-by-seven photo of Orlando Bloom pasted on the inside of the door, Danica's mouth turned up at the corners. "The janitor can fix that sticky handle for you."

Julep wished she'd thought of that earlier. "Okay. Tanks for your help."

Did she just say "tanks"?

I am too stupid to live.

"No problem." If Danica heard the error, she ignored it. She flipped a lock of hair over one shoulder. "Oh, here." She dug into the pocket of her brown suede backpack. She handed Julep an envelope. "It's an invitation to my Halloween party. Now that we're too old to trick-or-treat, it'll be something fun to do on Halloween night."

Too old to trick-or-treat? Julep had no idea there was an age limit.

"Come if you can." Danica began backing away.

"Wait," Julep said. She wanted to make sure she understood what was happening here. Danica was asking her—Julep Antoinette O'Toole, a.k.a. Julep Spew-Up—to come to her party as a *guest*? Was this a joke? What if she was inviting Julep because she needed some dweeb for the dunk tank or an extra bod to help her clean up? But how exactly do you ask something like that?

"I have to go. My number's on the card so you can RSVP. . . . Hey, I wonder what *those* initials stand for."

Perplexed, Julep lifted a shoulder. She had no idea. Her brain could barely process the events of these last three minutes.

"Anyway, there's going to be a prize for the best costume. It's gonna be a—"

The tardy bell rang, drowning out the rest of Danica's sentence.

"You'd better hurry. You're late." She straightened the front of her white denim miniskirt while trotting backward down the hall. "And so am I!"

Still reeling from everything that had just taken place, Julep reached for her math book and folder. She slammed the locker shut. Before disappearing into Mr. Meyer's English classroom, Danica called back to Julep, "Hey, Julep, I can relate to goal number three."

That was the one where Julep had promised not to eat so much chocolate.

"I should have made that one *after* Halloween," Julep answered.

Danica waved. "C.Y.L."

"C.Y.L." Julep wiggled her fingers.

Swapping secret code farewells with Danica Keyes.

Too weird for words.

Julep could hardly wait for second-period English. It was the first class of the day that she had with Bernadette. In the few minutes they had to settle in before the tardy bell, Julep huddled over Bernadette's desk and told her co-best friend how Danica had stopped to help open her uncooperative locker. As she listened to the story, Bernadette's mouth dropped open so wide Julep could almost count all of her bottom teeth.

"She said I shouldn't worry about the egg salad 'cause she got sick at camp last year, and then she said I should sue Calvin for reading my journal in front of everybody," finished Julep. "How about that?"

Bernadette was speechless.

"I almost forgot. She gave me this." Julep unzipped her backpack and whipped out the party invitation.

Bernadette read it. Three times. "Wow," she said, delicately turning the card over and over. "Wow."

"It came completely out of the blue."

"So." Bernadette shoved her glasses up her nose. "I guess this means we aren't going T.O.T-ing together."

Julep grimaced. "Is that okay?"

Bernadette tipped her head and bit a fingernail.

"I don't have to go the party," Julep said quickly. "It's no big thing." Which was true. It wasn't a big thing. It was a HUGE thing.

Julep wanted to go to Danica's party more than she wanted to eat or breathe or get the mother-of-pearl watch at Mulberry Lane. But she couldn't hurt Bernadette. No. Julep needed to be able to go to the party guilt-free. Clenching her fists, Julep gritted her teeth and waited for Bernadette to grant her permission.

Please say I can go. Please say it. Say it.

You're killing me here.

"It's Danica." Bernadette nodded. "Of course you have to go."

Relaxing her fists, Julep smiled. Bernadette Reed was such a warm, caring, unselfish friend. She was fortunate to have someone so understanding in her life.

"What costume are you going to wear?" asked Bernadette. "It says here the best costume wins a prize."

"I know. I've got a million amazing ideas," she said.

Actually, Julep didn't have a single idea, amazing or otherwise, but she didn't want Bernadette knowing that. Her co-best friend would take charge and pressure her into being something Julep didn't want to be, like a sea turtle or a spotted owl (Bernadette was into saving wildlife). While Julep appreciated Bernadette's commitment to the environment, she wasn't sure she wanted go to Danica's party as an endangered species.

Julep realized Bernadette was staring at her expectantly. She was waiting to hear some of the "amazing ideas."

"I . . . uh . . . I have to narrow them down," Julep stuttered. "I have so many."

"Well, it's great you get to go. Great. Really great."

Though the words were kind, the tone was strange. Julep got the impression Bernadette wasn't nearly as thrilled for her as she pretended to be. She could hardly blame her. Julep was ditching her best friend on Halloween to go to Danica's party. If their roles had been reversed, Julep would have been upset, too.

"You know"—Julep bit her lip—"the invitation doesn't say I can't bring a friend."

Bernadette was still holding the card. She glanced down. "It doesn't say you can."

"I could ask. Besides, it would be so much more fun with you there," said Julep.

"Thanks, but no." Bernadette held up a hand. "It'll look like you're begging."

Popular people hated beggars. That's not how the system worked. You had to be chosen. Once a girl started begging, or got someone to beg on her behalf, she immediately dropped off the popularity radar screen.

"Maybe she'll invite you, too." Julep tried to cheer up her friend. "Maybe she just hasn't gotten around to giving you your invitation yet."

"Sure." Bernadette's pursed lips slid up the side of her cheek. She held out the invitation, and Julep took it back, sliding it into her English notebook so she could look at it later during class. For a minute, neither girl said anything. Julep coughed and shifted her weight from her right foot to her left. Bernadette twirled a strand of hair around her finger. Julep was relieved when, thirty seconds later, the tardy bell rang, and she could escape to her seat.

A while later, Julep went to the back of the classroom to sharpen her pencil. Bernadette came up behind her to do the same.

"It's so strange," Bernadette said, watching Julep crank the sharpener. "Danica Keyes suddenly invites *you* to her party? I wonder what she wants."

Julep lifted a shoulder. She tried to pretend the thought had never crossed her mind, though it was all she'd been thinking about for the past half hour.

"I mean, she's never invited you to anything before. Only last year, she did everything possible to keep you out of her Girl Scout troop. . . ."

"She did not." Julep's fingers tightened around the crank, propelling it faster. "The group was full. They had, like, a dozen girls already. . . ."

"Uh-huh," said her co-best friend in a way that indicated she wasn't buying it.

Suddenly, Julep saw herself encased in a clear fiberglass booth. Stuck on a swaying bench perched over a pool of cold, dingy water, she was clinging to the ropes holding the bench in place and crying for mercy. No one would help her. Calvin Kapinski was cocking back his arm, aiming the beanbag at the target above Julep's head.

Blinking away the image, Julep swung around to face Bernadette. "She probably only invited me to—"

"Man the dunk tank." Bernadette sighed, biting the end of her pencil.

Bang! Calvin's beanbag hit the red-and-white circle dead center, and a second later, Julep was swallowing a mouthful of cold water. Even submerged, she could hear the goslings laughing.

That did it.

"I'm not going," Julep announced.

"Are you kidding? You have to go."

Julep was starting to get a headache. "But you just said—"

"That's why you have to go. To find out what she wants."

"I'd rather not know," muttered Julep, picturing Jillian, Kathleen, and Betsy lining up at the dunk tank for their turn at her.

Yet a part of her *did* want to know.

Danica had been so friendly when she had helped Julep open her locker. She had sympathized with her over the E.S. incident. Why, she had even remembered Julep's list of goals.

Nobody would be that nice just so they could dunk you—would they?

Maybe Julep was being too negative about this whole thing. What if inviting Julep to the party was Danica's way of finally choosing her? No more confidential compliments in the bathroom, kind whispers on the fly, or private conversations in an empty hallway. Maybe now Danica was ready to officially make Julep a friend.

"It *is* possible."

"What is?" pressed Bernadette.

"Oh." Julep blushed, not realizing she had said it out loud. "I was thinking that Danica . . . I mean she could want to—"

"What?"

"Be friends."

Bernadette snorted. And it wasn't a little grunt, either. It was so enormous that even the kids in the front of the class heard it. Everyone turned around to see who was mimicking a sick pig.

Angry and embarrassed, Julep yanked her pencil out of the sharpener and hurried back to her desk. There was no need for Bernadette to get nasty about things. True, she hadn't been invited to Danica's party, and Julep was very sorry about that. But that didn't give Bernadette the right to imply that someone like Danica would never choose someone like Julep as her friend. Bernadette was just jealous; that was all. Julep was, at long last, being summoned to join the head goose and the goslings. It might even happen today.

Julep could see herself strolling through the cafeteria, chatting and laughing side by side with the most beautiful and popular girl in the sixth grade. "Julep, that is soooo funny," Danica would say after every clever thing Julep uttered. "And you're such a good writer, too."

"She *is* a good writer," Betsy would echo from somewhere behind them.

"She sure is," Kathleen would say. "Don't you think so, too, Jillian?"

"Absolutely. I can't believe I hit her with my flute."

Not that Julep would need to eat lunch with them every day, because she *did* like hanging out with Trig and Bernadette. Maybe once a week, so everybody in first lunch could see that Julep was an important person. Okay, twice a week. How about Mondays, Wednesdays, and Fridays? That seemed fair.

But Danica didn't ask Julep to eat lunch with her that day. In fact, she passed right by Julep's table ten minutes into first lunch without even a glance in her direction. Bernadette, who hadn't said a word to Julep (or snorted) since third period, watched Danica go by with a satisfied smirk. It was as if she was saying, "See? I told you so."

Julep ignored her.

"What's with you guys?" Trig could feel the tension.

"Nothing," snapped Julep.

"Nothing," clipped Bernadette, pulling the top off her lemon yogurt so hard that little bits of yogurt flew across the table and hit Julep in the neck.

"Sorry," mumbled Bernadette as a frowning Julep cleaned herself off with a napkin. "I just know she's up to something."

"Why? WHY?" Julep threw the napkin on the table. "Why does she have to be up to anything?"

"Who?" asked Trig, glancing between them.

Bernadette ignored him. "Because—and no offense here—but you did barf your lunch all over the gym floor." She stirred her yogurt the required twenty-two times, then continued.

"Then there was that thing about your crush on Orlando that *everybody* heard. . . ."

"So?" Julep felt her scalp starting to itch.

"You're not exactly gosling material, if you know what I mean."

"Who'd want to be?" Trig asked.

"How do you know what I am? Maybe I am. As a matter of fact"—Julep puffed out her chest—"Danica said she thought my list was sweet. She said she liked the way I wrote."

"That's it!" Bernadette pointed her white plastic spoon at her. "That's what it is. She wants you to do some homework assignment for her. I knew it. I *knew* it!"

"She does not." Julep made a face. "All she did was invite me to her party. And you can't stand the fact that she picked me over you."

Bernadette gasped in horror and turned her whole body to the right so she wouldn't have to face Julep. Countering, Julep stuck her chin in the air and swung to the left. Bernadette Reed was such a cold, unfeeling, selfish person. What had she ever seen in her?

"This is pleasant," Trig said after several minutes of silence. "I never thought I'd see the two of you arguing over the head goose and her goslings."

"I'm not arguing," said Julep.

"Me neither," spit Bernadette.

Trig shoved the last of his jumbo hot dog in his mouth. "Glad we got that cleared up."

"I'll bet a week's worth of ice-cream sandwiches that Danica's up to no good," growled Bernadette.

"Mint chocolate chip is my favorite," retorted Julep.

"Strawberry banana is mine."

"So? What are you telling me for? You're gonna lose."

"Am not."

"Are too."

"Seems to me, Julep," drawled Trig, "if you're going to that party, it's your brother who's gonna lose."

Julep clamped a hand to her mouth. Cooper!

If she broke their pact, her brother would tattle to Harmony about the unauthorized borrowing of her sweater. Julep would end up being grounded for a couple of weeks and be forced to miss Danica's party. Everything would be ruined.

"Guess he'll get stuck trick-or-treating with your sister, huh?" asked Trig, unaware of the real problem facing her.

"Yeah," Julep tried to say lightly. "Guess so."

Don't panic, she told herself even as her heart picked up speed. *You'll figure out a way to handle Cooper. Nothing will keep you from going to Danica's party. Nothing will stop you from becoming visible to the whole world.*

Julep imagined herself gliding into Danica's home wearing the most spectacular costume anyone had ever laid eyes on. She wore a brilliant white satin gown with long, flowing sleeves that fell past her fingertips and a train of lace that trailed eight, no, ten feet behind her. Two sweeping, gossamer wings hovered above Julep's shoulders, just barely lifting her satin shoes off the floor. The wings were lit from within their filmy covering by tiny lights that sent out waves of color, turning from pink to red to gold and back to pink again like the fiber-optic Christmas tree her mother put up every year. On her head, Julep wore a crystal tiara (very much like Miss America's but a whole lot bigger) intertwined with delicate pink roses. Ribbons of gold glitter highlighted a once-wild mop of hair now tamed into perfect auburn corkscrew ringlets.

Danica rushed to greet her. "Congratulations! You're the winner of the best costume contest, Julep."

"But I'm the first one here," Julep said modestly, batting long eyelashes layered in silver glitter.

"It doesn't matter. No one else could possibly have a better costume than you," Danica replied, offering Julep an eight-foot trophy, a sixty-inch big-screen HD TV, and her eternal friendship. Then, pausing to look at Julep, really *look* at Julep, Danica asked, "How come I never noticed you before?"

It would be an incredible moment for Julep, a turning point in her miserable middle-child existence. Nothing and nobody was going to make her miss it.

10 Life's Little Surprises (Part II)

Dropping her backpack on the bench inside the front door, Julep took the stairs two at a time. She was anxious to begin brainstorming costume ideas. As wonderful as her angel daydream was, Julep knew it was just that—a fantasy. Fiber-optic wings, if they existed at all, would come under her mom's category of Too Expensive, as would a long satin gown and a tiara that dwarfed Miss America's crown. Julep would have to come up with a costume that was just as extraordinary and would get the same response from Danica but cost virtually nothing.

It was going to be a challenge.

At her doorway, Julep automatically lifted her left foot to prepare for the usual three quick hops that would get her across the creeping carpet A.F.A.P. (as fast as possible) and to the safety of her bed.

What was this?

The dog-doo carpet was different. It was a slightly lighter shade of brown, and the usual spots—the pizza sauce, the green swirl of ink near her desk, even the black goo in the corner—were gone! Her eyes darting from side to side, Julep could make out the faintest outline of one or two stains, but that was it. As her eyes traveled upward, Julep was in for more surprises. The snot-green walls were now neon orange. The paint was so vivid it seemed as if all four walls were throbbing. Or maybe that was her head. Julep was relieved to see her daisy curtains had replaced Cooper's crusty plastic blinds. But the soft, buttercup-yellow daisies on the white taffeta did not match the pulsating walls.

"What do you think?" Her dad was behind her. "I steam-cleaned your carpet, hung your curtains, and painted. Mom told me apricot was your favorite color."

"It is," she replied, though Julep didn't see how anybody could confuse fragile, airy apricot with a shade of orange that burned brighter than the sun.

"I know it's a little bold." He read her mind. "It was lighter in the can. It was such a great bargain. They had it on the half-price table at the hardware store, and I couldn't pass it up."

Why? She winced. *Why couldn't he have passed it up?*

"It's called Apri-Hot. Get it?"

Julep rubbed her temple. She got it, all right. Although a better name would have been Apri-Not.

"Your mom and I thought you deserved something special for trading rooms with Cooper."

I sure didn't deserve this.

"So what do you think?"

"I think . . . I think . . ." For the first time that day, Julep turned to look at him. Her father had a streak of orange paint across his chin. The front of his gray shirt was stained with sweat and a few more splotches of Apri-Hot. His cheeks were flushed, probably from moving her furniture around and pushing the rented steam cleaner that had, no doubt, taken a chunk out of their tight household budget. It was clear that Julep's dad had worked all day to give her a new room, one that she would love as much as her old one. How could she possibly tell him how she really felt?

"Mint Julep?" He was waiting. "Do you like it?"

"Like it? I . . . I love it," she said, wrapping her arms around him so he wouldn't see the lie in her eyes.

"Be careful when you go in there. The paint isn't quite dry." He patted her back. "I'll push your furniture back against the wall tomorrow. Keep the windows open, or you'll get light-headed."

"Huh? Oh . . . oh, yeah." Julep did feel dizzy, but it had nothing to do with paint fumes.

An hour later, Harmony found her younger sister sitting cross-legged on her bed. Julep was hunched over her journal, her mop of wavy hair hiding her face.

"I heard it was orange." Her sister whistled, glancing around. "But I had no idea."

"It's not so bad once you get used to it," said Julep, lifting her head.

Harmony caught sight of her sister in a pair of pink-framed sunglasses and broke out laughing.

"Hey, it works." Julep giggled, realizing how silly she must look wearing them indoors.

Still chuckling, Harmony went on her tiptoes to try to see over the top of Julep's journal. "Secret stuff?"

Julep brought the book to her chest, "No," she said warily. She didn't mind telling her sister what she had been writing about, but she didn't want Harmony to think it was acceptable to sneak a peek at her journal. It wasn't.

"I'm thinking up a costume for Danica's Halloween party."

"Danica?"

"Danica Keyes." Julep played it cool. "She's the most popular girl in school."

"Keyes, Keyes," she mulled. "Does she have an older brother named Bryce?"

"I . . . uh . . . don't know."

"I know why that name sounds familiar. Isn't she the girl who wouldn't let you in her Girl Scout troop last—"

"Nooooooo!" Julep interrupted. What *was* everybody's problem with this topic? "They were full. There were at least twenty girls who wanted in. She couldn't help it."

Harmony played with the tasseled end of a long braid. "So what are you gonna be?"

Julep tapped her gel pen against her teeth. "Maybe a ballerina." She had a practically new black leotard and pink tutu in her closet.

"That's right. You still have that outfit from when you flunked out at Miss Pauline's School of Dance."

"I did not flunk out." Her teacher had simply suggested that she might do better in another area, such as pottery or sewing or anything where you couldn't accidentally get your head caught between the ballet barre and the wall while trying to prove you had the smallest skull in the class. "I have an extra bone in my foot," Julep rushed to explain. "I couldn't dance."

"That's for sure," said Harmony. She pointed a finger at Julep before turning to go. "Just remember, no borrowing."

"I don't want to borrow anything, but I do need . . ." Julep paused, unsure if this was the right time to ask. Soon, she was going to have to beg her sister to take Cooper T.O.T-ing. Julep knew she was taking a big risk asking Harmony before she had really thought out what she wanted to say. But if she did it now, Harmony might say yes out of sympathy. After all, Julep was being forced to live in the Chicken Coop (now with new and improved blinding orange walls).

Harmony was waiting. "What?"

Julep crossed her toes and took a gamble. "I can't take Cooper trick-or-treating now, you know, because of the party. And I was wondering if you would—"

"No." Her sister's blue eyes flashed. "I'm going to Marielle's party."

"Come on, Harm," whined Julep. "You could take him out for an hour and then go to the party."

"So could you."

"No, I can't. The party at Danica's starts at six thirty. It doesn't even get dark until five thirty. If I take Cooper T.O.T.-

ing, I won't get back until six thirty. Then I have to get into my costume, and Mom has to drive me over to Danica's, and she lives way over on Blackhawk Road by the golf course. I won't get there until seven thirty or eight, and by that time, the whole thing will be almost over. Please, Harmony? Can't you do it this one time?"

Her sister stared at the ceiling. "I don't know. . . ."

Julep felt a spark of hope. "I'll never ask you for another favor as long as I live."

"I doubt that."

Julep clasped her hands in front of her, widened her amber eyes, and made her lower lip quiver. "Pleeeeeeease."

Harmony sucked in her cheeks. "Do my yard chores for two weeks?"

"Sure." That was easy.

"Clean my hairbrushes."

Julep's body trembled at the thought of yanking her sister's long hair out of a bunch of fungus-ridden hairbrushes, which, she was certain, had not been cleaned since the turn of the century.

"Deal," Julep said. She could endure a few cooties if it meant being free to go to Danica's.

"And . . ."—her sister was still thinking—". . . twenty bucks."

"Twenty dollars!" Julep flung her pen at her. "Are you serious?"

Harmony ducked, and the pen went past her head to bounce off an Apri-Hot wall. "If you don't want me to do it . . ."

Growling, Julep scooted off her bed and went to the closet

to get her elephant bank. She popped off the bottom and shook the bank until its contents fell onto her mattress—two five-dollar bills, three ones, five quarters, a nickel, and three pennies. "It's all I've got at home," she mumbled. "Take it or leave it."

Harmony took the fourteen dollars and thirty-three cents. The transaction had cost Julep more than she'd anticipated, but it was worth every leaf she'd have to rake, every strand of dead hair she'd have to pluck from a grungy brush, and every cent she owned to change her life forever. Now Julep would have to come up with a way to convince Cooper to go along with the plan. It was going to be tricky. His first name may have been the first six letters of the word *cooperate*, but that word sure wasn't any part of the boy she knew.

Julep knew she would have to choose her words carefully. She knew she had to make Cooper think it would be more fun to T.O.T. with Harmony than with her. She knew he would have to believe the idea was his and not hers. What she didn't know, what Julep couldn't possibly have known, was that while the two girls were deep in negotiations, they were not alone. Just a few feet outside Julep's bedroom door crouched a spy. A Froot Loop–stacking, jewelry-box-wrecking, mischief-making, seven-year-old spy.

And he had heard every word.

Dear J:

I RSVP'd to Danica tonight. It took me forever to get up the nerve to call. And then she wasn't even home. I left a message. I said I could come to her party. Then I forgot to leave my name, so I had to call back. I.A.S.A.D.!!

Next problem: Cooper. I think I am going to wait until the last minute on Halloween night to tell him Harmony is taking him T.O.T.-ing. He'll be mad, but there won't be much he can do about it. If he decides to tattle to Harmony about the sweater, it will be too late for my parents to ground me THAT night. At least I hope so. Keep your fingers crossed!

Here's what I've come up with so far for costume ideas:

- ◎ a die (as in one of a pair of dice)
- ◎ ballerina
- ◎ ladybug
- ◎ ~~Hilary Duff~~ (Danica will probably be her)
- ◎ the solar system
- ◎ ~~marshmallow~~ On second thought, A.A.F. (Do NOT remind people of E.S. incident.)
- ◎ poodle (I've got the hair!) WOOF!

111

I'm still working on it. I know, I know, I have to hurry.
Halloween is 6 days away.

Bernadette says she isn't mad anymore, but I can tell she is still
upset. She didn't call tonight, and she ALWAYS calls on Tuesday
nights after her oboe lesson. I think she is worried I will go to the
party, turn into a gosling, and forget all about her. T.W.N.H.!

   C.Y.L.,

      Julep

Julep's Secret Decoder Page
THIS IS A J.O.Z. (JULEP ONLY ZONE)

I.A.S.A.D.:   I Am Such A Dingleberry!

A.A.F.:   Avoid All Food

T.W.N.H.:   That Would Never Happen

**IF YOU'RE READING THIS,
PREPARE TO BE HUNG BY YOUR TOES!**

11 A Big Idea

Using only the tips of her toes, Julep set the swing in motion. Tipping her head back, she closed her eyes so that she could feel the sensation of gliding forward and back. Julep wrapped her fingers around the chain that suspended the swing from the ceiling of their back porch. And held on.

It was early evening, and Julep could hear the frogs singing their *Brr-roke* song. It was almost November, and there were only a few frogs left in the chorus now. Soon they would bury themselves in mud or leaves or burrow into the ground to go into torpor, a state of dormancy similar to hibernation. Julep had read all about it last year in science. Amphibians were ectotherms. That meant they depended on the sun to heat and cool their bodies. In winter, frogs slowed down their activity, heart rate, and metabolism in order to survive the cold temperatures. It all made sense scientifically. But emotionally, it was much harder. Julep couldn't help feeling a sense of abandonment when the last frog stopped chirping. If only spring weren't so far off. If only she didn't feel so alone.

Back and forth, back and forth, Julep swung, trying to shake off the sadness that had enveloped her. But it was no use. Danica's party was twenty-three hours away, and Julep still did not have a costume. For days, she had turned her brain upside down and shaken it, and yet not one single amazing idea had spilled out. Her mother had suggested she go as a princess (fab idea *if* she was five years old). Her dad said she'd make a great computer monitor (being stuck in a cardboard box all night was not her idea of fun). "Wear your yellow turtleneck," offered Harmony. "You could be a pencil. That wavy hair of yours is the perfect eraser head."

Real funny. Gag-o-matic.

Nobody in her family knew how critical this party was to her. Nobody understood that to a squish-squashed, misunderstood middle child, being noticed wasn't just something; it was *everything*. And, for the first time in her life, somebody important was finally paying attention to her. It had happened again that very morning. At the beginning of first period, Mr. Wyatt had sent Julep to the office to pick up some math assignments he had left with the secretary to copy. While Julep was waiting for Ms. Holcomb to finish up in the copy room, Danica's dark head had popped up from behind the main counter.

Julep nearly fell backward into a fake rubber tree.

"Oh, hi," said Danica, standing up.

"Hi," gulped Julep, shaking a clump of Spanish moss off her elbow. "You're . . . uh . . . here."

Of course, she's here, you dingleberry!

"I mean, you work here." Julep corrected herself.

"I'm the first-period TA." Danica reached over the secretary's desk for a stapler. She popped open the metal stapler and began loading it with staples. "And it isn't as much fun as you'd think. Ms. Holcomb actually makes me work."

"Sorry," mumbled Julep.

"Did you need something?"

"Ms. Holcomb . . . she's . . . copies . . . making." Cringing at her horrible grammar, Julep began to play with a piece of loose Formica at the end of the counter.

Danica snapped the stapler shut and put it back on Ms. Holcomb's desk.

"Um . . . did you get my RSVP?" Julep ventured.

"Yeah," Danica said absently. She was pawing through the secretary's top drawer.

"Thanks for . . . uh . . . inviting me," Julep said loudly, looking around at the empty room. Again, there were no witnesses.

"I was wondering if you were having a . . . a . . ." Julep flicked the Formica back and forth.

Just spit it out, will you?

Julep took a deep breath. "Are you having a dunk tank at your party?"

Glancing up, Danica frowned. "A dunk tank? No. Why? Did Jillian say we were? She loves those things. I hate them."

"Me, too." Julep clasped a hand to her heart.

No dunk tank.

Yippee! Yahoo! Hooray!

It was all Julep could do not to leap into the air. Now she could go to Danica's party without worrying if she was going to be Calvin's next victim. Or anyone else's, for that matter.

Julep had one more question for Danica. She was going to ask Danica if it would be okay to bring Bernadette to the party. Julep would not beg, of course. There would be absolutely no begging involved. It would just be a question. A normal, simple, nonpleading question.

"Danica, do you think—?"

The phone on Ms. Holcomb's desk jangled.

"One sec," said Danica. "If I let it go for more than two rings, Ms. Holcomb has a cow." She picked up the receiver. "Heatherwood Middle School. Student TA speaking. How may I help you?"

Danica sounded so professional. Julep leaned on the counter and tapped the white Formica with her fingers while she waited for Danica to finish taking a message. She would ask her, very casually, very coolly, if she could bring a friend to the party. She wouldn't name names, so in case Danica said no, nobody would get hurt.

Julep was still waiting for Danica to hang up when Ms. Holcomb returned. The petite secretary plopped a stack of papers in front of Julep and snapped her gum. "Here you go."

"Thank you." Julep picked up the pile of assignments.

Ms. Holcomb signed Julep's hall pass and handed it to her.

"Thank you," Julep said again, hugging the papers to her chest. She didn't move.

The secretary peered at Julep. "Is there something else?"

"Well . . . I'm . . . uh . . . no," sighed Julep, never taking her eyes off Danica. "Nothing else."

"Then you may go back to class."

Slowly, Julep trudged to the door. She took twenty-two baby steps, but when she reached the door, Danica was still on the phone. Julep held the door open with her back to let two kids in, hoping it would be just enough time for Danica to finish her conversation. It wasn't.

Ms. Holcomb was staring at her, so Julep had to let the door swing shut behind her. As she walked away, she could see Danica's dark head still bent over a memo pad.

Julep never got another opportunity to ask Danica about bringing Bernadette to the party. She felt guilty, but there was nothing more she could do. Bernadette hadn't expected to go anyway. She had said it was all right for Julep to go alone. Why, she had even encouraged it. And Julep knew now that no matter what, she *had* to go. It was worth the risk. For a flicker of an instant, Invisible Girl had appeared. Danica had seen her. The time had come for everyone else to see her, too. But if Julep didn't come up with a terrific costume, if she didn't win the prize, then she would vanish once more, perhaps never to reappear again.

Shivering, Julep hugged her peacoat around her and slid her hands into her pockets. But she did not stop swinging.

The screen door opened, and Julep's mother leaned out. "Don't forget, your dad and I have the museum fund-raiser tonight."

She had not forgotten. Harmony was going to be babysitting them, which meant Julep would be on cinnamon-toast-and-chocolate-milk duty all evening. W.A.N.

Her mom inspected her. "Everything okay?"

"Yeah."

"Can I swing with you for a bit?"

Julep moved over to make room.

Her mother buttoned up her woolly cardigan. "Frogs are almost done for the year."

Julep dropped her head onto her mother's shoulder. "I know."

After they had swung for a bit and listened to the frogs sing, her mom said, "Sorry about your room, hon. I'm really, really sorry."

"It's okay," muttered Julep. "I'm getting used to the Chicken Coop."

"I didn't mean swapping. I meant that ugly color your dad painted it."

"Apri-Hot? You should see it at night." Julep was relieved she wasn't the only one to think it should have been called Apri-Not. "The walls glow."

"I am so sorry about that," her mother said again. "It was supposed to be a reward, not a punishment. If you can wait a couple of weeks, just until payday, you and I will go pick out another color, okay?"

Happily, Julep agreed.

Mother and daughter kept the swing going, neither of them lifting their toes off the wood. Neither of them wanting to leave. The sun was setting beyond the fir trees, a rosy pink glow splitting the layer of high clouds. A lone mosquito buzzed around Julep's left ear, attracted to the glow of the porch light. Digging her hands deeper into her coat pockets, Julep felt the crinkle of paper under her fingertips. She brought out Bernadette's article on dust mites and unfolded it. As Julep stared at the page on her lap, an interesting idea began to seep into her brain. It descended on her, the idea did, the way fog rolled into the Snohomish valley on a brisk fall morning—silently, deliberately, magically. It was clever. It was fun. It was, unquestionably, original. Nobody else, she was certain, would have anything like it.

"Mom, can I have some stuff from your craft cabinet, you know, like a couple of Styrofoam balls and a few pipe cleaners?"

"Sure. Is it something for school?"

"I'll need some butcher paper, too."

"I only have blue."

"It'll do." Julep put down a foot to stop the swing.

Popping up, she hurried across the porch, but before she got to the door, Julep swung around and ran back to give her mother a swift kiss on the cheek. "Thanks, Mom."

"You're welcome, but what are you going to do with all the—?"

The screen door was already banging shut.

A teeny-weeny bug had just given Julep a very big idea.

Who would have ever thought that she, Julep Antoinette O'Toole, M.M.M.C., would be glad she'd gotten stuck in the Chicken Coop?

6:03 P.M.   Mood: joyful

NEWS FLASH!

Dear J:

I've got it! I've come up with the perfect costume. Ready? I am going to be a dust mite. I know it's weird, but you have to admit that no one else will be wearing anything like it. Plus, I can make it myself at home for free. I'm going to put tons and TONS of glitter on it. I'll be like a Las Vegas showgirl dust mite. P.F.G.

Gotta go and make my fantabulous costume before Harmony starts yelling for cinnamon toast and chocolate milk (she's babysitting us tonight). Yuck—o.

    C.Y.L.

    Julep, S.T.B.V.M.C.

P.S. I cleaned out two of Harmony's brushes today. The tangled globs of dead hair were bad enough, but then there was

this white, scabby gunk on the brush that took forever to wash off. T.D.F.W.

Julep's Secret Decoder Page

UNAUTHORIZED ENTRY!   GO AWAY!

P.F.G.: Prepare for Greatness

S.T.B.V.M.C.: Soon To Be Visible Middle Child

T.D.F.W.: Too Disgusting for Words

MAY WHOEVER READS THIS
BE CURSED WITH PERMANENTLY SMELLY FEET!

"Julep, we're leaving now."

"Wait!" Julep was in the middle of ransacking her drawers. She'd found her pink ballet tights and a pair of too-small navy tights with tiny white polka dots. But it wasn't enough. She raced out of her room. "Mom, I need four more legs."

Her mother, who was at the top of the stairs, turned. "Legs?"

"Do you have any old stockings?"

"Uh . . . I suppose. Check my bottom drawer. Don't take them unless they have runs in them," she called after her daughter. "And no fighting."

"We won't." Julep would be too busy working on her costume to waste time arguing with her siblings.

In her mom's dresser, she found a pair of charcoal-black panty hose and a pair of bright-red tights, both with runs. Yes! She now had all eight legs. She was ready to make her costume. First, Julep unrolled the sky-blue butcher paper across her carpet, cut it in half, and placed one half over the other. She knew it wouldn't be wise to simply start snipping away without a pattern for the body. She needed something to trace around—a circle. A big circle. But what could she use?

"Oh," Julep said out loud, hopping to her feet. She ran to the bathroom and grabbed the beige oval rug off the floor. She dragged it into her room and placed the rug on top of the layers of butcher paper. Then, using a dark blue crayon, she traced around it. Julep lifted the rug and cut out the pair of paper ovals. She also cut two foot-long rectangular strips to connect the front and back of the dust mite's body at the shoulders. Once the strips were stapled in place, Julep sprayed both ovals with lots of blue glitter glue. Julep drew a circle on each grapefruit-sized Styrofoam ball with her permanent black marker and filled it in. She searched through her bottom dresser drawer until she found an old black knit ski cap that she hardly ever wore. Gluing the two Styrofoam balls onto the brim of the cap for eyes, she attached the two black pipe cleaners into the knit above the balls. Julep bent the tips at the ends to create a pair of antennae. Julep also cut out a paper mask to fit over her nose and around her eyes. She decorated the mask with swirls of blue paint and more blue glitter. Julep stuffed each of the stockings with newspaper and stapled two pairs to the front oval (red and pink) and two pairs to the back oval (black and navy). At last, after nearly two hours of work, she was ready to try on her dust-mite outfit.

Carefully Julep lifted her arms and slipped the paper costume over her head. It moved down a few inches, then got stuck. She tried wiggling the paper ovals loose, but that didn't work. She attempted to slowly bring her arms down, but a ripping noise stopped her.

This is just great.

With her arms straight up over her head and the paper cutting off her oxygen supply, Julep was trapped inside the big blue dust mite. She thought a couple of legs must be tangled above her head. Slowly Julep pushed the costume up. She heard another tear. Julep tasted paper. And the glitter was starting to smell like the tuna sandwiches at school after they'd been sitting out for an hour.

Julep reached around the side of the costume until her hand grasped a pair of stockings. She flung them apart, and the costume came loose, falling onto her shoulders. She took a big breath of fresh air before adjusting the straps. Then Julep put on the knit cap. She had to readjust antennae that had gotten twisted. Also, one of the eyes hung lower than the other, but because it was glued on, it would have to do. Finally, she secured the paper mask onto the back of the cap with masking tape (it took her two tries—the first strip of tape got tangled in her hair).

Julep went downstairs to look at herself in the full-length mirror on the back of the laundry-room door. Harmony was sitting on the floor of the family room, folding a load of clothes. Julep ignored her amused expression. Her own reflection in the mirror, however, was another matter. It could not be ignored. Julep had prepared herself. She knew there would be no long, flowing, white satin gown; no shimmering tiara intertwined with roses; no gossamer fiber-optic wings—but she had not expected to look like . . . like . . .

"You look like one of those guys in Blue Man Group," burst out Harmony. "What are you supposed to be? A mutant blueberry? An overweight bluebird? Oh, I know. . . . You're a sick octopus."

Julep whirled around to tell her sister to shut up, and one of the Styrofoam eyes fell off her head. It rolled across the floor toward Harmony, who reached to pick it up. "Think fast," she quipped, tossing the thing back to Julep. "Well, whatever you are, it won't matter now."

"What?" Julep didn't get it. And Harmony knew she didn't get it.

"Don't you have something to confess?" asked her sister, digging out one of Cooper's soccer T-shirts from the pile of laundry beside her.

"No," answered Julep, spinning to see what the back of the costume looked like in the mirror. Maybe if she sprayed more glitter glue on it . . .

"Nothing?" prompted Harmony. "Are you sure?"

What was her sister up to? Whatever it was, Julep was determined not to rise to the bait. She didn't want to get into trouble for arguing.

"You want me to make you some cinnamon toast?" Julep asked politely.

Harmony wasn't deterred. "You have nothing to say about my black angora sweater?"

Suddenly, Julep had to go the bathroom. She crossed her ankles and bounced a few times.

"You took it after I told you not to, didn't you?"

"Well, I . . . not exactly . . . I mean . . ." Julep kept dancing in place, her eight floppy legs bobbing in time to her rhythm.

"Don't bother lying. I found out you took it"—Harmony shook out the navy-blue shirt—"from a very reliable source." She turned the shirt toward Julep, and the white block letters emblazoned across the back revealed the truth: SUPER COOPER.

Julep stopped bouncing.

Rats!

He had done it to her again. What had she been thinking—trusting a seven-year-old, pain-in-the-rumpus little brother who couldn't keep a secret any longer than you could chew the flavor out of a wad of bubble gum?

"I wouldn't plan on going anywhere for Halloween." Harmony gloated, laying the shirt flat on the floor to fold the arms across the back.

Deflated, Julep fell into the nearest chair. *Riiiiiip*. Somewhere on her body, paper was tearing. It didn't make much difference now.

Invisible Girl was back.

And this time, she was staying for good.

12 JULEP'S JUSTICE

"Cooper Maynard O'Toole." Julep flung his bedroom door open. "I want to talk to you right now!"

The room was dark. The light from the hallway cast eerie shadows from Julep's pipe-cleaner antennae on the far wall. Back in her old room again, Julep felt a tug of longing. The buttercup-yellow walls, the bay window, the polished birch wood floor—once they were hers. Now they were wasted on an evil-scheming, secret-spilling, room-stealing, ungrateful little brother.

He wasn't going to get away with it. Not again. This time, Cooper was going to pay for his crime. This time, merciful parents would not be enough to save him. Oh, no. He would be tried and convicted in the Court of Julep. Found guilty by a jury of Julep's peers (Bernadette and Trig, naturally), he would be sentenced to four years of hard labor, for that was how long she figured she'd be grounded for borrowing Harmony's sweater. Cooper would have to follow all of Julep's rules. And there would be a *zillion* of them. Cooper would have to:

- Stop chewing food with his mouth open and showing the contents to her (yuck-o).
- Quit burping, farting, and spitting (all similar armpit sounds would also be forbidden).
- Buy Julep a new jewelry box: the new deluxe two-tiered model with working ballerina.
- Walk by himself to school. No. Wait. Walk in front of Julep to school, scattering rose petals in front of her. Much better.
- Serve her breakfast in bed every Saturday (meaning he had to bring the waffles to her room, not put them in her blankets).
- Stay out of her room, out of her journal, and preferably out of her life!

Julep glanced around in the darkness. Too bad he wasn't here so she could hand down her sentence. She was about to leave when she spotted a tiny white foot hanging off the side of the bed. It might be Frosty, his giant stuffed polar bear, or it could be . . .

Julep crept closer. It was Cooper, all right. He was lying crosswise on his bed, holding one of his Spider-Man action figures. He looked so cute and cuddly and peaceful sleeping that way. But she wasn't fooled. This very moment his devious mind was probably dreaming up new ways to torture her.

"Hey." Julep tugged on his foot. "Wake up."

"What?" Her brother lifted his head. Still groggy, he shaded his eyes against the ray of light coming in from the hallway and caught sight of the antenna shadows on the wall.

Julep opened her mouth to demand an explanation for breaking their pact.

Before she could say a word, Cooper started screeching, "Monster. It's a monster!"

"No." She tried to explain but got a kick in the knee for her efforts.

"Get away . . . get away from me!"

"Ouch."

"Help, Julep!" He was thrashing around and punching the air.

"I'm . . ." She was trying to tell him to quit screaming for her, that she was right there beside him, but he wasn't giving her a chance.

"Get away, you big, ugly monster," Cooper continued shrieking as he pummeled Julep's body with the full force of his fists and feet. She could hear her dust-mite body tearing.

"Oh, for Pete's sake, Cooper . . . ow . . ." One of his wild punches caught her in the stomach. Julep stumbled backward over a pile of toys, lost her balance, and hit the floor. Her elbow smashed into something hard. "Ohhh," she moaned.

Cooper fell off the end of the bed but kept right on screaming. Scrambling to his feet, he slid across the shiny floor, knocking over a bunch of stuff on his way. *"Julep! Somebody! Help me. . . ."* Her brother zoomed out the door, trailing a pair of navy tights with white polka dots behind him.

Watching two of her eight legs fly down the hall made Julep giggle, though each hiccup of laughter sent a ripple of pain through her stomach. She had certainly gotten her revenge, even if it hadn't gone quite the way she'd imagined.

Score one for the miserable, misunderstood middle child.

Still sprawled on the floor, Julep watched a dented Styrofoam eyeball roll slowly past her foot.

"You should have seen him tear out of the room at mach speed." Julep chuckled into the phone. She was cradling it against her shoulder, stirring together two teaspoons of sugar and one teaspoon of cinnamon in a cereal bowl. "He ran into the bathroom and hid in the shower. It took Harmony almost an hour to get him to come out."

Bernadette squealed.

"At last I got him," Julep cried out in victory. "I got him good. It feels fab-U-lous. "

"I'll bet," cheered Bernadette, who had experienced her share of Cooper's Capers, as she called his annoying tricks, jokes, and pranks. "But what about your dust mite costume?"

"It's ruined. But it's all right. It was pretty lame to begin with anyway."

"Don't worry. You have time to come up with another costume. Read me your list."

"I didn't have a list," admitted Julep. "The dust mite was my one and only original idea."

"I could come over tomorrow and help you think of some-thing else—"

"No point to it," Julep broke in. "I'm not going to Danica's party."

"Not going?" Bernadette was aghast.

"You're the one that said Danica only invited me because she wanted someone to do her homework."

"I was mad," she muttered. "I'm sorry. You should go, Julep. I'm dying to know what her house looks like inside. You just gotta go and tell me everything. And I mean everything."

"You don't understand. It's not that simple anymore."

"What do you mean?"

Grabbing the slice of browned bread that popped out of the toaster, Julep placed it on a plate and cut it in half diagonally. "I borrowed a sweater from my sister without asking, and she's gonna tattle to my parents when they get home tonight. So I'm officially toast." Julep glanced down at the bread under her fingertips and grinned.

I'm making toast, and I AM toast. You are what you eat.

Julep spread a thin layer of butter on the toast before sprin-kling it with the sugar-and-cinnamon mixture. "It would take a miracle for me to go that party. A miracle."

And as anyone could tell you, miracles did not happen to Invisible Girl.

Julep wanted to change the subject. Now. "So are you going T.O.T.-ing with your cousins?" she asked Bernadette.

"Maybe. I heard Mrs. Wiley is giving out giant Hershey bars, so I might go up to Bridle Trails and do the circle."

"Giant Hershey bars?" That did sound fun.

"Trig said I could go forking with him, but I don't know."

"What *is* forking, anyway?"

"You don't know what forking is?"

Julep was getting tired of people asking her that question.

"It's the most ridiculous thing," said Bernadette. "I'm sure a boy thought it up—it's that stupid. See, you get a whole bunch of—"

"Bern," Julep cut her off. "I have to go."

"What's wrong?"

"It's Cooper."

Her friend let out a hearty laugh. "What's he done this time?"

Julep stared at the pale, grape-juice-stained face of the boy standing in the kitchen doorway. Cooper was holding Fred against his heaving chest.

"He's having an asthma attack," Julep croaked. "A bad one."

13 A Real Scare

Harmony!" Julep yelled, throwing the phone onto the counter.

Yanking open the top drawer of the cabinet next to the pantry, Julep reached inside for her brother's emergency inhaler. She checked the top to make sure it was loaded with a canister of medication. It was. She shook it several times. Julep removed the cap from the inhaler and snapped on a fresh spacer tube.

"What?" Harmony appeared at the door. "You're supposed to bring me my toast and milk in the family room . . . ohmygosh," she choked, realizing what was happening. "Is he all right?"

"He will be," Julep said confidently, handing the inhaler to a heavily wheezing Cooper.

"What are we supposed to do?" Harmony's voice went up a full octave.

"Stay calm." Julep shot her a warning look. "I know what to do. Give me a good exhale first," she reminded her brother.

Cooper let out a ragged breath, put the inhaler to his lips, and tipped his head back a bit. He squeezed down on the top of the can to release the first puff of medication.

Harmony was kneading her fingers. "What's that?" she asked nervously when a sound resembling the horn of a birthday-party blower came out of the inhaler.

"He's inhaling too fast," said Julep. "Slow down, Cooper. That's better."

Once he lowered the inhaler and gave her a nod, Julep began the count. "One, two, three, four . . ."

At ten, her brother exhaled and coughed several times.

"He doesn't look good," Harmony said, biting her fingernail.

Julep noticed Cooper's shoulders were crunched up his neck, and his eyes were brimming with worry. She needed to get him to relax.

"You're gonna be fine." Julep steered her brother to one of the kitchen chairs. She sat down and pulled him into her lap. "Just like at school, remember? We can do this."

"Yeah . . . huh . . ." He tried to smile.

Harmony was pacing around the butcher block. "Should I call the doctor? Should I call Mom and Dad? Maybe I should start the humidifier."

"That's a good idea—the humidifier," said Julep, though she would have agreed to anything to get her sister out of the kitchen. Panic was infectious. And when paired with asthma, it could be disastrous. Cooper was frightened enough. She did not need him catching Harmony's fear and getting worse. The moment Harmony left the room, Julep felt her brother's body loosen up. She felt more at ease, too.

"Looks like Fred's tail is torn," Julep said. "Want me to sew it up when we're done?"

Cooper hugged his bunny tighter. "Huh . . . okay."

A minute or so later, Julep had her brother take a second puff on his inhaler. "Good," she said when he finished. "I can hear your lungs opening up already."

He turned to search her eyes, to try to decipher if she was being completely honest with him. She forced herself to grin and prayed he couldn't see the worry behind it.

"Okay, okay." Harmony flitted into the kitchen. "I turned on the humidifier in Cooper's room. Now what?"

"It might not be a bad idea to call Mom and Dad," Julep said. To Coop she added, "Not because I'm freaked or anything, but because they'd want to know what's going on."

"Oh, my God," screeched Harmony, the phone in her hand. "I forgot their cell phone number!"

Calmly, Julep gave her sister the number, along with a raised eyebrow with the hope that Harmony would get the subtle message and chill out.

"Let's count crazy," Julep said lightly as Cooper went for his third puff. "Ten, one, nine, two, eight, three, seven, four, six, five, and breathe. . . ."

"They aren't answering," cried Harmony, circling the kitchen table with the phone attached to her ear. "They're not answering!"

The clock on the microwave read 9:26. Their parents would

be inside the museum at the benefit auction now, so they'd probably turned off their cell phone. It would be another hour or more before they turned it back on for the ride home.

"Try again in a few minutes. Let's pound you," Julep said to her brother. He leaned over the mosaic kitchen table so she could begin hitting his back with her fist.

"Should we call nine-one-one?" asked Harmony, twisting the ends of her hair.

Cooper stiffened in Julep's arms.

"Let's give the medicine time to work," Julep answered firmly. "Coop, what do you think?" She'd started to ask her brother what he thought might have caused the attack when a horrible thought dawned on her.

Cooper's asthma could have been brought on by many things: pollen, dust, fur, feathers, exercise, cold weather. Or it could have been triggered by . . .

Julep swallowed hard.

. . . too much excitement.

About an hour and a half ago, a ninety-three-pound blue dust mite with rainbow legs and a loose eyeball had scared the pudding out of the child now sitting on her lap gasping for air.

This time the cause of Cooper's asthma was no mystery.

It was all Julep's fault.

Following her sister's advice, Harmony brought the humidifier downstairs and set it up in the tiny powder room off the front hall. Sitting on top of the red-carpeted toilet seat cover, Julep continued pounding Cooper's back to loosen the mucus in his lungs while he inhaled the moist air from the humidifier. Yet twenty minutes later, his wheezing had improved only slightly.

It was close to ten o'clock. Harmony had tried several times to reach their parents without success. It was possible the battery on their cell phone had gone dead. There was no telling when their mom and dad might come through the door. They could come through the door in one minute or one hour.

Julep weighed her options. She could keep pounding Cooper's back and let him continue sucking in the moist air from the humidifier. She could have him take another puff on his inhaler. She could turn on the shower in the main bathroom to really get some steam going to clear his lungs. These things might work. But they might not. The girls could call 911, but it would frighten Cooper. If he *was* getting better, the trauma of having paramedics burst in and whisk him away to the hospital might actually make his asthma worse. On the other hand, if he wasn't getting better, doing nothing was unwise.

It was such a big decision, and right now Julep felt so small. The knowledge that she had caused his asthma attack was making her feel even worse. How could she have been so thoughtless?

Stop. You can't think about yourself right now. You have to focus on Cooper.

"Jules." Her brother was trembling. ". . . huh . . . I'm scared."

"I know," she whispered, rubbing his damp hair.

Me, too.

As another coughing fit racked his wiry body, a tiny, clammy hand clasped on to her wrist. Julep saw that his fingernails had a bluish tinge. When he was done coughing, she lifted him off her lap and gently placed him on the toilet seat.

"Jules . . . huh . . . don't leave. . . ."

"I'm not going anywhere," she said, stepping into the hallway. She crooked her finger, and Harmony, who was wiping her eyes with a tissue near the front window, came scurrying over.

As quietly as she could, Julep said, "We can't wait any longer. We need to get Cooper to the emergency room, and we need to do it now."

14 Coming Up for Air

I'm glad you called," Gran said, when Julep opened the back door for her. Wearing her blue jeans and white Keds, their grandmother's trim figure zipped past the girls and into the kitchen. She dropped her huge, dirt-brown leather purse onto the counter.

"Cooper's ready," said Julep, stepping into the family room to signal her brother that it was time to go.

On the couch, Cooper slumped down in his jacket.

Julep went to kneel beside him and tie his shoes.

"I don't . . . huh . . . wanna go."

"I know you don't."

"I want . . . huh . . . Mom." His voice broke.

"Cooper, this is really important. You don't want to get worse, do you?"

He didn't answer.

"The doctor's going to give you some different medicine. Then tomorrow you'll feel better, and you can go trick-or-treating."

He humphed and looked away. "I know you're not . . . huh . . . taking me out . . . for Halloween."

She was astonished. "What?"

"I heard you . . . huh . . . and Harmony . . ."

Julep fell back on her heels. "Well, that was . . . it was . . ." She sputtered for a good excuse but changed her mind. Cooper deserved the truth. "I'm sorry," she said. "I guess we both broke the pact, huh?"

He looked at her funny. "What? I . . . huh . . . didn't break it . . . huh . . ."

"You told Harmony . . . never mind," she said, seeing the confused expression on his face. It was not worth upsetting him further. "I promise I'll take you trick-or-treating tomorrow, if Mom and Dad don't ground me, I mean."

"How do I know . . . huh . . . you'll keep it . . . huh . . . this time?"

"You'll have to trust me." She looked him straight in the eye and asked softly, "Will you?"

Cooper munched on his lower lip for a few seconds before giving her a reluctant nod.

"Then you'll go with Gran?"

He flopped his legs. "All right."

Bundling a blanket around her brother, Julep tucked Fred under her arm and walked Cooper to their grandmother's silver Nissan Pathfinder. When she leaned over to strap him in, he put his arms around her and wouldn't let go.

"Can I go, too?" Julep asked Gran, who was leaning over the driver's seat to put her purse on the passenger side.

"You should stay," her grandmother said, glancing behind her to where Harmony was sniffling into a shredded tissue.

"Okay," Julep said, prying her brother's arms from around her neck. "I'll be here when you get back," she whispered to Cooper. "You can sleep in my room if you want."

"Love you . . . huh . . . Jules."

"Love you, too, Pooper-Scooper. Try to relax. You're still really tight."

"Easy for you to . . . huh . . . say." He rolled his eyes.

"I'll call you from the hospital, girls," said Gran, shutting Cooper's door after Julep stepped away. She patted Harmony's arm, then gave Julep a peck on the forehead. "You did the right thing."

The two sisters stood side by side and watched their grandmother pull out of the driveway. They waved to Cooper. He gave them a tiny wave back, his pale-blond head barely visible above the window. The car rolled to the end of the block, signaled a left turn, and disappeared. For several minutes, neither Harmony nor Julep moved from the end of their drive.

Julep felt uneasy, as if waiting for a hurricane to strike. She couldn't see the oncoming storm, but she could feel it in the air, could feel that it was about to come roaring into her life in some violent, frightening way. And she hated the helpless feeling that came with it.

Please, God, let him be all right.

"He forgot Fred," Julep said suddenly, realizing she was still holding the bunny. "I told Coop I'd sew his tail."

"I'll do it," said her sister quietly.

Nodding, Julep took three shallow, quick breaths the way you do when you are about to start crying but are trying to keep it together. "It was my fault," she whispered to herself.

"No, it wasn't," said Harmony. "If anything, you saved him. I've never paid attention to all that stuff Mom and Dad did with him. I didn't know what to do. I'm glad you were there." Her voice sounded so much different from the one she usually used when talking to her younger sister; there was no mocking tone, no superior attitude, no hint of irritation.

Harmony reached for Julep's hand, or, perhaps, it was the other way around.

It didn't matter.

Somehow, it no longer made a difference who was the first-born child or who was more loved by their parents or who had to sacrifice the most stuff for Cooper. Julep knew she had wasted too much energy thinking about those things already, and she didn't want to do it anymore. Julep wove her fingers through her sister's and held on tight.

She slowly exhaled, and the warmth of her breath created a wispy fog cloud in the chilly night air. She watched the cloud fade away, only to be replaced by another. Then another. On the third cloud, something occurred to Julep. Air wasn't always invisible, was it? The truth was that everybody forgot about air until it connected with microscopic bits of dirt and dust and pollen to form a cloud. Then you saw it. Then you remembered how important it was to your very survival. Then you appreciated it.

Julep's life was sort of like that, too. Everybody forgot about Invisible Girl until they needed her. Then, and only then, did they see her.

So? Is being needed such an awful thing?

Julep had to admit it felt good to have people depend on you—to count on you to be brave enough to give up your room, to run to you when monsters attacked, to look to you for strength in a crisis. It felt good to be needed, even for a little while.

Julep glanced down at the worn stuffed bunny under her arm.

She was beginning to understand now.

Julep *was* air. But she had made one critical mistake in her thinking. She had believed that no one could see her, but actually, she was the one who couldn't see the truth. All along, she had been visible to those who loved her. All along Julep had been visible to everyone except herself.

10:41 P.M.   Mood: frantic

EMERGENCY JOURNAL ENTRY

Dear J:

I'm scared. Terrified is more like it. Cooper had a big asthma attack tonight, and Gran is taking him to the emergency room. My parents weren't here when it happened, and we're still trying to reach them.

If I hadn't frightened Cooper with my dust—mite costume, the whole thing wouldn't have happened. Harmony says she was pretty sure he was wheezing a little after he came in from shooting baskets with Kenny this afternoon, but I think she is only saying it to make me feel better. But I don't feel better. I can hardly sit still. I hate waiting.

Please, God, take care of Cooper.
Please heal his asthma.
Please let him come home.
He can have anything he wants of mine. I promise.

Love,

Julep

P.S. Harmony finally got ahold of our parents, and they are on their way to the hospital to meet Gran. What a relief! Now we wait.

Did I mention I <u>HATE</u> waiting?

15   Miracles

I could make some new cinnamon toast for you," offered Julep, watching her sister slide the cold piece of bread off the plate and into the garbage can.

"I'm not hungry," Harmony said. "You want anything? I don't mind making cookies."

"No," Julep said sharply. The mere thought of having to eat a meteorite made her ill.

"I wish they'd call. How long has it been?"

"An hour and fifteen minutes since Gran left and two minutes since the last time you asked how long it's been." Julep wiped her tired eyes.

"If you want to go to bed, I can wait by the phone."

"I'll stay awake with you." Julep collapsed into a kitchen chair. She scooted a few pieces of mail out of the way so she could lay her head down sideways on the table. The mosaic tabletop felt cool against her left ear.

Harmony slid into the chair across from her. She put her elbows on the table and rested her chin in her palms. "I've decided something."

"Yeah?" Julep yawned.

"I'm not going to tell Mom and Dad about the sweater."

"I'm broke," Julep warned.

Harmony traced a finger around a triangular piece of powder-blue china set into the grout of the mosaic tabletop. "No charge."

Julep frowned. If she wasn't after cash, then what *did* her sister want for her silence?

"You're in the clear." Harmony read her expression. She reached to rescue an eight-by-twelve white envelope that was starting to slide off the table. "Stuff like what happened tonight makes you realize what's important. And what isn't."

That was certainly true.

"Of course," her sister continued, "if you would have said what the sweater was for in the first place when you asked to borrow it, I might have agreed."

"You would *never* have said yes," protested Julep, watching her sister stand the envelope up against the sugar bowl. "You said no borrowing, no exceptions. Those were your exact words."

"You didn't say it was for this." Harmony slid both the bowl and envelope toward her.

Cautiously, Julep lifted her head. From within a clear plastic window on the front of the envelope a familiar face grinned out at her.

"Hey, my school photo."

"Hey," mimicked Harmony, pointing at the envelope. "*My* sweater."

Of course! How could Julep have been so careless? In all of her plotting and scheming to get out of, and back into, the house undetected while wearing the stolen sweater, she had totally forgotten that her school photo would reveal her crime. Why, from the moment the photographer had snapped the shutter, Julep had been doomed. Cooper *had* been telling the truth. He had not betrayed her. He had not broken their pact. Julep had tattled on herself. Didn't it just figure?

"I wish they'd call. How long has it been?"

"Don't go there."

A minute later, Harmony asked, "You're not really going to Danica's party as a dust mite, are you?"

"Nope."

"Thank goodness, because you looked ridiculous. I do have a decent reputation at school, you know, and I'd like to keep it that way. If Danica's older brother saw you in that getup . . ." Harmony crossed her eyes. "So what costume *are* you going to wear?"

"Not going. I promised Cooper that if I wasn't grounded, I'd take him trick-or-treating."

"I doubt that'll happen." Harmony was absently flipping through the rest of the mail on the table. "It's supposed to dip down into the forties tomorrow night. I'd say Coop's not going anywhere."

She was right. Cold weather could aggravate asthma symptoms. The doctor was unlikely to give Cooper the go-ahead to run around outside in a flimsy Spider-Man costume for a couple of hours so soon after such a major asthma attack.

"He's going to be crushed," Julep said.

"There's nothing you can do about it. He'll have to wait until next year."

Julep felt sorry for her brother, but another thought, a very different thought, was already creeping into her brain. Did she dare even consider it? Was there really a chance that she might still be able to go to Danica's after all? Julep felt awful for even thinking such a thing while her brother was in the emergency room fighting for his life. She forced herself to put all thoughts of Danica and the party out of her mind. But it wasn't easy. Things like that—tantalizing, fascinating, tempting things—somehow always had a way of sneaking back into her brain.

Julep wondered what the prize for best costume would be. Movie tickets? A tub of red licorice? Maybe a fourteen-karat gold ankle bracelet. Wouldn't that be something? The nicest piece of jewelry Julep owned was an opal butterfly necklace with a cracked wing. Wouldn't it be great if she won a fourteen-karat gold ankle bracelet that matched one of Danica's? It would show Calvin Kapinski and the rest of the world that Danica Keyes and Julep O'Toole were close friends. No one would dare read her journal out loud or make fun of her ever again. Julep would wear her magic ankle bracelet forever, even after she became a famous writer.

"Julep, wake up. Julep?" Harmony was shaking her shoulder.

Blinking, Julep slowly sat up. When had she dozed off? And how long had she been asleep? The right side of her neck was stiff, and there was a small pool of drool on the mosaic table next to where her mouth had been. Yuck-o.

"Gran just called," her sister was saying.

Gran? That's right. They were still at the hospital.

Her heart suddenly slamming against her chest, Julep squinted. "Is he all right? What happened?"

Her sister's pinched face broke into a grin. "Coop's gonna be okay."

Thank you, God.

Thank you. Thank you.

Tears of relief, stress, and exhaustion flooded her eyes. Julep tried looking up and blinking a few times to make them go away the way her grandmother had taught her. But it didn't work. Too tired to fight, she gave in and let the salty droplets roll down her cheeks. It felt good to finally release her torrent of emotions.

Somehow, a tissue found its way into her hand.

Julep wiped her eyes and blew her nose. She was so tired. So very tired.

"They're going to keep Cooper until the morning, so Dad's gonna stay at the hospital with him," explained her sister. "Gran's bringing Mom home now. Come on, let's get some sleep."

Julep didn't need any convincing. She didn't think she could stay awake even one more minute. Not even the glow-in-the-dark, throbbing Apri-Hot walls would keep her up tonight.

Harmony yawned as they trudged up the stairs. "In the morning, we'll figure out a costume for you."

Julep nearly lost her balance. Had she heard right? Was Harmony actually going to help her?

It truly *was* a night of miracles.

"Well?" Harmony's breath tickled her ear. "What do you think?"

Julep took a hesitant step forward. Was the dazzling reflection in the mirror really her? Was it possible that Julep Antoinette O'Toole, Miserable Misunderstood Middle Child, had been transformed into a glittering, enchanted creature of the sea?

Yes!

Julep was going to Danica's party as a mermaid.

She ran her hand across the top of the V-neck turquoise leotard and felt the bumpy gold sequins beneath her fingertips. Swirls of gold sequins skimmed like waves across her chest and down the clingy sleeve of her right arm. The leotard was part of one of Harmony's old dance costumes. She had been a peacock in Miss Pauline's annual recital last year. The leotard was a few sizes too big for Julep. The neck kept sliding off one shoulder, but it didn't matter to Julep. It was still gorgeous.

For her body and tail, Julep's mom and Harmony had spent much of the afternoon huddled over the sewing machine, making a long wraparound skirt out of a few yards of turquoise knit fabric (with golden sparkles) Gran had donated from her remnant pile. Julep's mom had created several ruffles of fabric, sewing them to the back hem of the skirt. The ruffles fanned out behind Julep's heels to create her mermaid tail.

With a lot of help from her mousse, gel, and hair-spray collection, Harmony had managed to pull Julep's wild chunk of hair back and twist it into a bun. On her head, Julep wore a wreath of dried lavender, baby's breath, and white ribbons. It was another one of Harmony's treasures, from when she had won second runner-up in the Junior Miss Evergreen State Fair beauty pageant last summer.

Watching Harmony paint Julep's face with blush, mascara, and eye shadow, their mother said, "I think you're overdoing it on the makeup, Harmony."

"She's got to glitter."

"I don't know." Julep's mom shook her head at the long streaks of sapphire and aqua eye shadow that rimmed Julep's eyes.

"Come on, Mom, it's Halloween," begged Julep.

"All right, but that's enough," their mother said quickly when Harmony pulled out her magenta lipstick.

Julep couldn't stop gazing at herself in the mirror. It was her; yet it wasn't her. Transformed into a glamorous mermaid, she was sure to attract all kinds of attention from Danica and the goslings at the party.

"What an awesome costume," Danica would say, admiring Julep's ruffly turquoise tail.

"Awesome," Betsy and Kathleen would echo in unison.

"Don't forget, she's a good writer, too," Danica would remind them.

Jillian shook her head. "And to think I accidentally hit her with my flute. . . ."

The doorbell rang.

"I've got this group," said her dad, grabbing the bowl filled with mini-Snickers bars. Soon, a joyful cry of "Trick or treat" filled the room.

Harmony spritzed more hair spray on Julep's bun. "You can wear your black ballet shoes from when you flunked out of Miss Pauline's—"

"I did not flunk out!"

"Whatever. Go get them. It's almost time to go."

"Thanks, Harm," Julep said, twirling one last time to see her tail sparkle in the mirror. "This is the best costume I've ever had."

"It's not bad, is it?" Her sister smiled. She pointed a blush brush at Julep. "Just don't get anything on my leotard."

Julep moved gingerly up the stairs. She didn't want to step on her back fin or mess up her hair. In her room, Julep slipped into her ballet shoes and headed back down the hallway. She was at the top of the landing when something made her glance toward the end of the hall. A red glow was emanating from Cooper's room. It was his Lava lamp. He always turned it on when he was feeling down. Julep glided to the end of the hall and peered inside.

Cooper was sitting in the bay window, holding Fred, whose tail Harmony had repaired the night before. His head resting against the glass, Cooper was staring down at the street. One of his windows was slightly open, and the sounds of children chattering and calling out to one another drifted up.

"Coop?"

Her brother was so intent on watching the scene below, he didn't hear her.

Or maybe he did hear her, and he didn't want to talk right now.

Padding away, Julep left him with his thoughts. On her way out, she stopped in the upstairs bathroom to check her costume one last time before leaving for Danica's.

Her reflection was so unbelievably perfect, from the flowing, sparkly turquoise fabric to her exotic makeup to the little tendrils of hair that curled around each ear. At last, all that Julep had hoped for was within her grasp. She was going to go to Danica's Halloween party, win the prize for best costume, and be adored by everyone who was anyone at Heatherwood Middle School. Everything Julep had longed for with every cell in her body was about to come true.

So how come she felt so crummy?

Because no matter how hard she tried to deny it, this was nothing more than your typical Cinderella thing. A mermaid costume might get you noticed for a little while, which was certainly nice. But after the party ended, once Julep had wriggled out of Harmony's leotard and washed off her colorful makeup, she would go back to being her old self; the same girl Jillian had bonked with her flute, the same girl Danica talked to or ignored, depending on her mood. If Julep had to work this hard to get the attention of the head goose and the goslings for one single night, how was she possibly going to impress them every day at school? There weren't enough clothes in Harmony's closet for that.

"What's the point?" Julep sighed, taking a long look in the mirror. Eyes the color of a Bermuda sunset seemed to throw the question back at her. Standing here, Julep realized her eyes were the only thing about herself she recognized. And it scared her.

It had taken Invisible Girl eleven long, painful years to appear. Finally she was visible to herself and her family. If she got distracted and started focusing on the wrong things, Julep worried she might start to fade away again.

Why did it matter so much what Danica thought of her? Wasn't it enough that people she loved most in the world could see her? Wasn't that something?

It was more than something. It was *everything*.

"*That's* the point," she said to her reflection, who quickly agreed.

Now it was all starting to make sense. And Julep knew what she needed—no, what she wanted to do.

Holding her lavender wreath tight against the top of her head, Julep hopped downstairs as fast as her turquoise mermaid tail would allow.

16 A Historic Halloween

He's coming," Harmony hissed from the kitchen doorway. "Get ready, everybody."

Chortling, Julep squirmed as she stood shoulder to shoulder with Bernadette. Behind them, candy was heaped high on the mosaic table: mini–Three Musketeers, Milky Ways, Snickers, M&M's, Baby Ruths, Butterfingers, Life Savers, along with assorted bubble gums, lollipops, jawbreakers, Tootsie Rolls, and packages of Gummi Bears. Julep had never seen so much candy in one place. Bernadette had placed Mrs. Wiley's oversized Hershey bars on top of the mountain of treats.

They hadn't counted their haul, but Julep's mom estimated the three girls had gone to about seventy-five houses, so, combined, Harmony and Julep's bags added up to more than one hundred fifty pieces of candy Bernadette had wanted to include hers, too, but Julep's mother had insisted she keep her own candy. "This is plenty," she'd said.

A few hours earlier, Julep had broken the news to Danica that she wasn't going to come to her party. "My brother's been sick, and he can't go trick-or-treating," she explained on the phone. "Bernadette and I thought we'd go out for him, so I'm re-RSVP-ing to tell you I can't make it after all."

"Okay." Danica didn't sound devastated.

"By the way, I looked up *RSVP* on the Internet," Julep rushed on, not wanting to be impolite.

"Yeah?" Her tone hadn't changed.

"Remember, you were wondering what the initials meant."

"I was?"

"Come on, Danica," Betsy was saying in the background.

"Anyway, it's French." Julep tried to hurry. "I can't pronounce the words, but it means 'please respond.' A lot of times, people RSVP only if they are coming, but they're supposed to call even if they aren't coming. So that's what I'm doing. I'm RSVP-ing to say I can't come. Sorry."

"It's okay," Danica said lightly. Almost *too* lightly.

"Thanks for inviting me. . . ."

"I have to go," Danica said. "We're going to start a game."

"Sure."

"Bye."

"C.Y.—"

Click.

Julep never got a chance to tack on the *L.*

She hoped the most beautiful and popular girl in the sixth grade understood her reasons for not showing up, but if she didn't, then Julep could accept that. Turning off the phone, she twirled on her heel to find her sister shaking out a couple of tall kitchen garbage bags.

"I'm going with you guys," Harmony announced.

"You are?"

"You paid me to go T.O.T-ing, and that's what I'm doing. However, I would like to make it clear that I am *not* shouting 'Trick or treat,' nor am I wearing a costume. Got it?"

"Fine with me."

And that had been that.

"He's here," Harmony said, flicking on the kitchen light.

Rubbing his eyes and tugging on the rear end of his Spider-Man pajamas, Cooper asked sleepily, "What's going on?"

Julep couldn't keep her knees or her feet still. "We have something for you." She stepped to her right, while Bernadette moved left.

"Whoa! Look at this." Cooper walked toward the table, his arms outstretched. "Wowee!"

"It's yours," said Harmony.

"No way."

"The girls went trick-or-treating for you," their mother said with a grin.

"This is *all* mine?" Cooper curled his fingers around a bunch of individually wrapped gum balls.

"Take it easy, kiddo. You get it in small amounts—two pieces a day, that's it."

"Ah, Mom . . ."

"Those are the rules."

"At that rate, he won't finish this until next Halloween," Bernadette said with a giggle.

Surveying the mammoth pile of candy, Cooper cocked his head.

Uh-oh.

Julep recognized that tilt. He was up to something.

"Mom?" Cooper asked innocently. "Uh . . . can I have a piece now?"

She held up a finger. "One. Then I'm putting the rest up in the cupboard."

"Okay." A devilish smile dancing across his face, Cooper climbed up on a chair. He stretched out and grabbed one of the giant Hershey bars off the top of the pile.

Everyone laughed, including their mom.

Julep could tell her mother was proud of her by the way she kept touching her heart and beaming at Julep from across the room. Her mom was in such a good mood she didn't even make Cooper put the big candy bar back. Julep was in such a good mood she didn't think about the prize that someone else was winning for best costume at Danica's. Okay, she thought about it once. But the look of gratitude on her brother's face was better than anything she could have won at some silly party.

Except maybe a fourteen-karat gold ankle bracelet.

Or a sixty-inch HD TV.

Or a diamond-studded tiara.

Cooper threw his arms around Julep's waist.

Then again, maybe not.

———

It was Sunday morning, the first day of November, and Julep was helping her dad make French toast for everybody. She dunked the bread into the bowl of whipped eggs, tapped it down with a fork to make sure it absorbed plenty of egg, and passed the bowl to her dad. He fished out the bread and plopped it into the pan. Julep loved the sizzle of steam that wafted up when the bread hit the hot pan. Holding the spatula, Julep kept her eyes on the clock. In two minutes, she would flip the slice of bread. Two minutes after that, she would scoop it out of the pan and onto the plate. Then they would start all over again.

"Is it done yet?" Cooper banged his fork against the table. "I'm starving."

"Take it easy, buddy," said their father. "It's coming."

"Can I have some of my candy?" Cooper squirmed in his chair.

"No, you *may* not," said their mother, taking a sip of coffee. "After we get home from church, I'll consider it."

Harmony buzzed into the kitchen, her hair pinned up. The tips were fanned out above her head, making her look like a rooster. "Have you seen the front yard?" she asked, opening the fridge door.

"It was still there last time I checked," said Julep with a giggle, flipping the French toast right on time.

"Cute," her sister snarled, pouring herself a glass of grape juice.

"Is there something wrong?" their dad asked, leaning back against the corner.

"Wrong?" Harmony squished her mouth up one side of her face. "No . . . I wouldn't say wrong, just different. Definitely different."

"Different how?" Julep pressed the next slice of bread down into the egg mixture so it would be ready for the pan.

"You'll have to see it for yourself."

Julep and her dad exchanged curious looks. Her dad took the pan off the heat and turned down the burner. Flinging the spatula on the counter, Julep hurried into the living room after him.

"Where are you going?" shouted Cooper. "I'm hungry now!"

Julep's dad unlocked the front door, swung it open, and motioned for her to go first.

In bare feet, Julep stepped out onto their front porch.

It was incredible. Spread out across the evenly cut grass were dozens and dozens of white stakes. Aligned in perfect rows, the stakes were spaced about a foot apart. They stretched all the way from the front of the house to the picket fence next to the sidewalk—more than thirty feet. Not one section of the lawn had been left untouched. Diagonal rows of stakes even veered off into the side yard. There were hundreds of them. Julep tried to count the rows but lost her place after thirty-two. The entire O'Toole front yard resembled a miniature cemetery, except that instead of tombstones the markers were . . .

Julep stepped farther out onto the porch.

They couldn't be. Could they?

Trig wouldn't have. Would he?

"What are they?" her dad asked.

Julep trotted down the stairs, knelt down, and pulled out a stake. She held up the end that had been in the ground. "Dad," she said, grinning at him through the white plastic tines. "We've been forked."

17 Frog Dreams

Using the toe of her right tennis shoe to push down the heel of her left shoe, and vice versa, Julep managed to kick off both shoes without having to untie them. What an awful day. She'd gotten Mali confused with Bali on the map quiz in social studies and ended up with a B minus. The janitor had spent the whole morning working on her locker, and still it was refusing to function properly. And, worst of all, The Borg had announced they were starting a new unit in PE: tumbling.

Just what her stomach needed.

W.A.N.

Her backpack hanging off one shoulder, Julep stopped in the kitchen for a handful of barbecue potato chips before heading upstairs. In her room, which was now painted Angelic Apricot—a normal shade of apricot—Julep dumped her pack on the floor. Sliding the zipper open, she began unloading books and notebooks. Julep had a lot of homework along with a humongous math test tomorrow. In fact, Bernadette should be calling any minute so they could study together via phone.

Munching the last of her chips, Julep tossed her math book

on her desk. She was about to reach for her favorite pink gel pen when she noticed a small black box sitting on her dresser. It was tied up with a shiny red ribbon—the kind that you could make curl by sliding it down one blade of a pair of scissors. Next to the box sat two white envelopes, side by side. One was short and square. The other was a long, business-sized envelope. Both had her name written across the front.

Julep chose the short envelope closest to the black box. She tore open the flap and pulled out a little white card.

> *Dear Julep:*
> *Here's a small reward for a big sacrifice. Hope you like it. Love,*
> *Mom and Dad*

Julep gently tugged on one end of the curly ribbon, and it fell away from the box. She lifted the lid. When she saw what was lying on the bed of cotton, Julep let out a cry.

Julep lifted the watch out of the box and slid the stretchy silver band onto her wrist. Pink, purple, and clear beads, along with silver roses, clinked together as she moved her arm. She lifted the oval mother-of-pearl cover to see the pearly face inside. Twelve tiny pink rhinestones in a circle winked at her.

Harmony. It had to be Harmony who had told their parents about the watch, for she was the only one who had seen Julep admire it at Mulberry Lane.

It was a wonderful surprise.

Eagerly, Julep opened the second envelope. But this time, there was no note inside.

Instead, it contained two five-dollar bills, three ones, five quarters, a nickel, and three pennies—exactly fourteen dollars and thirty-three cents.

8:18 P.M.   Mood: peaceful

Dear J:

I got an A minus on my math test. I studied so much I'm certain I blew a brain fuse. I.N.C.! So much for Goal #3 on my list. Things are back to normal with Danica and the goslings. Translation: I'm invisible to them. It's weird, but I've stopped noticing them as much, too. It's like they're there but not there. Know what I mean? Besides, if Danica can only talk to me when her friends aren't watching, how lame is that?

 Trig is still pretending he has no clue who forked my lawn. What a B.G.L.! The good news is my dad is happy because he was going to hire somebody to aerate the lawn (it means to poke holes in the lawn to let the air reach the roots). Who knew? I guess everything needs to breathe, even grass.

Cooper and I walked down to the pond tonight, but all of the frogs have stopped singing. I guess they are all tucked into their leaves, logs, and mud for the winter. I read that wood frogs in Canada and Alaska can survive winter temperatures well below freezing because their bodies make their own antifreeze. How freaky is that? Smart frogs.

Sleep well, frogs. Sweet dreams.

See you in the spring.

Love,

Julep Antoinette O'Toole, V.M.C.

Julep's Secret Decoder Page

ACCESS DENIED!
KEEP OUT!

I.N.C.:   I Need Chocolate

B.G.L.:   Big Goober Liar

V.M.C.:   Visible Middle Child (At last!)

WARNING!
THIS JOURNAL WILL SELF-DESTRUCT IN 10 SECONDS!

Turn the page to read
an excerpt from the next book
featuring the lovable Julep O'Toole!

Julep O'Toole:

Miss

INDEPENDENT

1 Hot Girl vs. Steamed Mom

Where on Earth did you get *that*?"

The brass-heart key ring slipped from Allison Gallardo-O'Toole's fingertips. Her keys hit the sandy-beige carpet with a *thplud*.

"This?" Julep glanced down at the plum shirt, where a swirl of gold barrel beads splashed the words HOT GIRL across the front. "It's an S.E. tee, Mom."

"A what-ee?"

Zipping her backpack, Julep shouted up the stairs, "Cooper! Let's go."

If her seven-year-old brother didn't get moving, they were not going to get to the corner of Bayview and Chenault on time. Last time they were late, her co-best friend Trig had found a rusty pair of hedge clippers and was turning the Ramplings' boxwood hedge into a French poodle. You never wanted to leave Trig Maxwell and his devious mind alone for more than eight minutes. Julep and her other co-best friend, Bernadette Reed, had timed him. Eight minutes was his limit. After that, there was no telling what he'd do.

It was clear Julep's mother was waiting for a more detailed explanation from her eleven-year-old daughter.

"It's a self-expression tee," said Julep. You had to be from another galaxy not to know about the latest fad. "They say things like SWEET STUFF and BRATTY TO THE MAX. Everybody is wearing them."

"You are not everybody."

Julep snorted. "I knew you were going to say that."

"Then you also know I am going to say there is no way you're wearing *that* to school."

Flipping a springy lock of reddish-brown hair behind one ear, Julep let out a frazzled sigh. No, she hadn't known that. When Julep had convinced her aunt Ivy to buy the shirt for her, she'd had a feeling her mother wasn't going to be thrilled about it. But Julep had not expected a complete parental meltdown. They were just words; two harmless, glittery, swishy words. What was the big problem-o?

Lately, her mother seemed to exaggerate every tiny thing Julep did. The other day, she'd grumbled for most of the evening after Julep had come home from Trig's house a few minutes late. The way her mother had laid into her you'd have thought Julep had been eleven days overdue instead of a measly eleven minutes. Then, yesterday, her mom had burst a few thousand blood vessels because Julep had forgotten to empty the dishwasher. It wasn't like she'd done it on purpose. She'd simply lost track of time turning Bernadette's foot into a rainbow. That's where you paint each toenail a different color of the rainbow. You know, the big toe gets red, the toe next to it is done in orange, and so on down the line with green, blue, and finally violet for the baby toe. In a real rainbow, yellow would be between orange and green, but then a person would have to have six toes like Calvin Kapinski (or so he claimed). Because one color in the foot rainbow has to go, everybody skips yellow because, well, yellow toenails?

Ew. Fungus among us.

Anyway, her mom had stripped Julep of her phone privileges for a whole week because she hadn't gotten her chores done on time. It was S.N.F. (so not fair).

Julep figured her mother's stressful job was partly to blame for her weird behavior. Allison Gallardo-O'Toole was the director of public relations at the Seattle Art Museum. She was in charge of all of the museum's publicity and special events. Whenever anything went wrong, her mother had to swoop in to do what she called "damage control." That meant reassuring the media and the public that everything was under control, even if, sometimes, it wasn't.

Tightening the laces of her tennis shoes, Julep told herself that once the Venetian-glass exhibit ended and people weren't milling too close to priceless, breakable art, her mom wouldn't be quite so touchy. At least, she hoped so. Julep didn't know how much longer she could stand her mother's uptight, easily freakable attitude.

"Julep, did you hear me?"

How could I not? She bit the words in half on her tongue before they could fly out of her mouth.

"Answer me, please. Where did you get that?"

She wished her mother would quit saying the word *that* as if Julep was sporting a dead possum on her chest. Straightening, Julep felt a tingle zip across the top of her skull. An itchy scalp was a sure sign she was starting to get angry.

Take it easy. Just get out the door without getting into another argument.

Julep ran her fingers through the front of her hair, pulling her thick wave of terra-cotta bangs straight up into the air. There was no sense prolonging it. Her mom was going to keep pestering her until she confessed.

"Aunt Ivy," she said.

Her mother slapped her palms together. "I knew it."

Then why did you ask?

"It's no big deal, Mom." Julep madly scratched her right temple. "Bernadette's mom just got her one that says SPOILED ROTTEN."

"Well, that certainly fits."

"It's a little big for her, actually," said Julep, missing her mother's point.

"What that girl needs isn't any more junk. What she really needs is someone to—" Julep's mom stopped when she looked into her daughter's questioning, amber eyes. "Never mind," she said quietly, bending to pick up her car keys off the floor. "I have a meeting to get to. I don't have time for this."

"And I do?" mumbled Julep.

"What did you say?"

"Nothing."

Julep's mom rubbed her forehead with the thumb and index finger of her right hand, a signal that her middle child was starting to give her a headache. "I don't know about your attitude lately, young lady."

My attitude? MY attitude? You are totally kidding me, right?

However, Julep did not dare utter a word. Some things you were not supposed to say because adults didn't want to hear the truth. They were what Julep called the taboo topics and had to be saved for her journal. Thank goodness for her journal! It was the one place where she could write what she was forbidden to utter out loud. Without it, Julep was certain she would have wilted faster than Mrs. Knudsen's Joseph's Coat roses. So many times Julep felt exactly like those flowers: curious and hopeful, but also fragile and temporary. Nobody knew, of course, except her journal. For that was the one place where she was free to be her best and *worst* self—the moody, goofy, lazy, stubborn, unreasonable, S.E.-tee-wearing Julep that wasn't allowed to exist in her mother's world.

Her journal didn't try to change her. It accepted her the way she was. It let her be. Without her journal to confide in, Julep was certain the petals of her spirit would shrivel up and blow away in the wind.

"*That* shirt," her mother said again, "is not appropriate for a girl your age. I'm not even sure if it's appropriate for someone my age."

"They're not meant for old people."

Big mistake. HUGE. She braced for the worst.

Her mother's lips tightened into a white line as she dug through her purse. Much to Julep's surprise, however, she didn't say anything.

This was ridiculous. It wasn't like Julep actually believed she was a HOT GIRL or anything. She wasn't a complete dingleberry. Nobody with eighty-seven freckles sprinkled over her face, a chest flatter than a Fruit Roll-Up, and hair that resembled a tumbleweed in a dust storm could ever be mistaken for a HOT GIRL. Yet that was the whole point of wearing it: to show everyone there was another side to her—a wild, unpredictable side.

If she was lucky, Julep might even get her picture in the What's In? section of the school newspaper. That was where they highlighted the latest catchphrases, fashion trends, music, and crazes going around on campus. Nelson Gibbs, who shot photos for the newspaper and yearbook, always had his digital camera with him in first-period math. Actually, he carried it everywhere. "You have to be ready for any sudden photo op," he'd told Julep when she'd asked him why he lugged so much heavy gear around all the time. "Plus, my dad will kill me if I leave my camera in my locker, and it gets stolen."

"Photo op?" Julep had wondered.

"Opportunity."

Wouldn't it be outrageous if today Julep was Nelson's photo op?

"Julep!" Nelson would call the moment she strolled into math class, his camera flash going off in her face. Before she could blink the spots from her eyes, a herd of photographers would start snapping away.

"Julep, over here," the paparazzi would shout.

"Miss O'Toole, turn this way."

"Julep, your outfit is amazing."

"Thanks." Julep would strike a supermodel runway pose, making sure not to trip over the cord to Mr. Wyatt's overhead projector.

"How does it feel to be voted Best Dressed Girl on Earth?"

"I'm thrilled, of course."

Twirl and pose. Pose and twirl.

"Julep, is it true you're going to Hollywood next week?"

"Well . . . yes. I promised ages ago to style Avril for the Grammys. But that's all I can say." She would raise her hands when pressed for details. "Please, no more pictures. I really must go. Mr. Wyatt is testing us on prime numbers today."

"Just one more pose? It's for the cover of Seventeen."

Well, maybe just one more—for the fans.

"Look this way, Miss O'Toole."

Pop. Pop. Pop. A new shower of flashbulbs would explode.

"Julep, over here."

"Julep!"

"Julep?" Her mother was waving a couple of one-dollar bills at her.

With a depressed sigh, Julep took her lunch money and stuffed it into the front pocket of her jeans. When her mom turned away, she slung her backpack over her shoulder and tip-toed like mad toward the front door. Cooper was on his own now. She was going to make her escape and she was going to do it guilt-free. After all, hadn't Julep almost always followed the rules? Hadn't she almost always done whatever her parents asked of her? So if, for once in her ordinary life, she wanted to wear something extraordinary, was that so horribly wrong? Was that such a crime? Was it too much to ask to let her have this microscopic fleck of joy?

She reached for the doorknob.

"Julep Antoinette O'Toole."

Apparently so.

When your parents use all of your names and dice them like fresh tomatoes, you're shish-kebabed for sure.

Julep dropped her hand first. Then her head. "Yeah?"

"You are not to be seen in *that* at school."

"But, Mooom—"

"Upstairs. Now. Move." Once her mother started barking like the Gunderfests' St. Bernard, she was past listening to reason. It was all over.

Steamed Mom: one. Hot Girl: zero.

Julep let her backpack slide off her shoulder and onto the floor. Stalking past her mother, she trudged up the stairs. Halfway up, she nearly got run over by Cooper, who was thundering down the steps. The whole right side of his pale blond hair stood at attention. "Where are you going, Jules? I thought we were late."

"I gotta change."

He snickered. "Told ya."

"Shut up. You've got four Cap'n Crunch squares on your chin."

"I glued them on with milk. I'm saving them for recess."

"Mom's gonna—"

"She knows. Wanna see where I stuck the crunch berries?"

"No!"

Cooper's topaz-blue eyes flashed. "I'm telling mom you said shut up."

"Go ahead." She continued on her way up. "Add it to the list."

This was so typical. Julep wasn't allowed to wear her S.E. tee, but the human cereal bar got a free pass out the front door.

Julep's brother and sister got away with everything. Julep's fourteen-year-old sister, Harmony, was popular, beautiful, smart, athletic, and talented. She was in the ninth grade at Snohomish High School. Harmony was, among other things, a JV cheerleader. Big woo. Julep didn't know why everyone treated cheerleaders differently, like they had some sort of superpower or something. This morning, Harmony had pranced into the kitchen wearing three layers of Sizzle Red lipstick and a white denim miniskirt so tight a Barbie doll would have had trouble squeezing into it. But did Julep's mother say a single thing about *that*? Nope.

Huh.

Maybe Harmony did have a superpower after all: parental mind control.

In her room, Julep wrestled out of the plum T-shirt. She balled it up and chucked it into the Black Hole. Her father had named Julep's closet the Black Hole, noting how stuff mysteriously got sucked into it never to be seen again—things like her souvenir Tigger bracelet from Disneyland, last year's social-studies book, a cheetah-print scarf, and one of a pair of tuxedo cat socks her grandmother had given her (Julep had, in her defense, found the other sock behind the dryer).

Furious, Julep stomped in a circle. This was a complete injustice. Wrong, wrong, and in every sense of the word, wrong. She was not a baby. She was eleven years old and perfectly capable of selecting her own wardrobe.

Flinging open the bottom drawer of her dresser, Julep began tossing shirts and sweaters in every direction. About to thrust her battleship-gray, authentic Irish, hand-knit sweater skyward, suddenly it dawned on Julep what was really happening. Clutching the sweater to her chest, she rose to her feet.

Things were beginning to make sense.

It wasn't her mom's stressful job that was to blame for what was going on. Nor was it the tight spandex shirt or the adorable swish of gold words. Her mother had gone nuclear because she didn't want to admit that Julep was grown up enough to make her own decisions. If she acknowledged that, then she would have to stop controlling Julep's every move. She would have to trust Julep.

Horrors!

No matter what her mother said, Julep knew she *was* old enough to decide what she should and could wear. And nobody was going to stop her from doing just that.

Rescuing the HOT GIRL tee from the Black Hole, she shook it out and threw it on over her head. A few minutes later, Julep glided down the stairs wearing her gray, hand-knit sweater with the wide sleeves that fell a good three inches past her fingertips. For the past two years, her grandmother had been insisting that Julep would eventually grow into the sweater she had brought back from Ireland for her. Not a chance. There was still room to fit two, maybe three, NFL football players in the thing. Perfect-o!

". . . I couldn't let her wear that to school." Already on the phone to Aunt Ivy, Julep's mother was cradling the phone against her shoulder. "Don't worry. I'll return it for something sensible."

Translation: something hideous.

"Hmm. Maybe something in a toasty brown? She *loooooooves* brown."

She haaaaaates brown.

Not that anyone ever asked.

Julep collected cereal boy from in front of the television and headed for the door. Gracefully, she swept past her mother and tossed the two stringed tassels on her sweater, which you were supposed to tie at the top of the V-neck, over one shoulder. Her mom raised one eyebrow as if to ask, "That's a pretty thick sweater for March, isn't it?" But all she whispered was, "Have a good day."

"I plan to," clipped Julep, her chin in the air.

Julep wore her HOT GIRL shirt to school. And she did it without disobeying orders. After all, her mom had forbidden her to be "seen" in the S.E. tee. So Julep simply kept her thick sweater on over the shirt so that no one would actually "see" her in it. It was a brilliant move, except that by the end of first period, Julep really *was* a hot girl—temperature-wise.

Springtime and chunky wool sweaters do not mix.

But the suffering was worth it.

Julep was tired of being told what to do. She had her own thoughts, opinions, and ideas. She had her own way of doing things. Why couldn't her mother understand that all Julep wanted was . . .

All she wanted was . . .

. . . what?

Julep didn't know. Still, she had a voice, even if she wasn't certain yet what she wanted to say.

A tiny bead of sweat trickled down the back of Julep's neck.

When Mr. Wyatt turned to write their math homework assignment on the whiteboard, Julep ripped a blank page out of the back of her notebook. She folded the piece of paper into an accordion and began fanning herself.

Air. She needed air.

Her bell sleeve fell down for the hundredth time that morning. Angrily, Julep pushed it back up to her elbow. She was mature enough to make her own decisions. And she was going to prove it to everybody. The sleeve slid down again. One hundred and one. If becoming independent meant sweating to death inside an enormous, gloomy-gray sweater that fifty sheep somewhere in Ireland had given their precious wool for, well . . .

Julep shoved her sleeve up.

. . . so be it.